I0634401

Henry Morley, Robert Southey

Roderick, the Last of the Goths

Henry Morley, Robert Southey

Roderick, the Last of the Goths

ISBN/EAN: 9783337105754

Printed in Europe, USA, Canada, Australia, Japan

Cover: Foto ©Andreas Hilbeck / pixelio.de

More available books at **www.hansebooks.com**

Companion Poets

RODERICK

THE LAST OF THE GOTHS

BY

ROBERT SOUTHEY

EDITED WITH AN INTRODUCTION

BY

HENRY MORLEY, LL.D.

EMERITUS PROFESSOR OF ENGLISH LANGUAGE AND
LITERATURE AT UNIVERSITY COLLEGE
LONDON

LONDON
GEORGE ROUTLEDGE & SONS, LIMITED
BROADWAY, LUDGATE HILL
GLASGOW, MANCHESTER, AND NEW YORK
1891

INTRODUCTION.

SINCE Chaucer's day until the year 1814 no poet
had produced a tale in English verse of nobler
strain than Southey's *Roderick*, first published in
that year. It is its writer's masterpiece in verse,
and the *Life of Nelson*, published but a few
months earlier, is commonly accepted as his
masterpiece in prose. He wrote these books
when in the fulness of his power, in his fortieth
year, and he was busy upon these books when he
was made Poet Laureate, in 1813. The writing
of Roderick was begun at Keswick in December
1809, and finished there in July 1814. The French
had entered Spain in 1807. In March 1808 they
took Madrid, where, on the second of the following
May a revolution broke out, and the French were
massacred. On the next day the whole province of
Asturias rose against the invaders. The French
were defeated at Vimiera on the 21st of August.
On the 21st of February 1809 the heroic defence of
Saragossa by Palafox ended with its capture by the
French; Cordova and Seville were taken in the
following November. In that year, and after it,
deep interest in the patriotic struggle drew all eyes
to Spain. It put new life and new significance
into the old Spanish romances of the struggle to
free Spain from the grip of the Moor, and caused
three poets to fasten upon the story of Count
Julian's calling in the invader, the overthrow of
Roderick, the last Gothic king, and the beginning
of the struggle for the freeing of the land from

5

foreign conquerors, and the establishment of
Spanish nationality. Walter Savage Landor's
play of *Count Julian*—which I have reprinted,
together with his *Gebir*, in one of the threepenny
volumes of the "National Library"—was begun
in 1810 and published in 1812. Walter Scott's
Vision of Don Roderick, reprinted at the close of
the last volume of these "Companion Poets,"
associated, Roderick directly with a vision of the
future, closing with the Peninsular War and the
success of the long struggle to free Spain from the
grasp of Bonaparte.

Southey in earlier life had visited Spain. He
had learnt its language, studied its history, and
delighted in its old romantic lore. Three centuries
of Gothic rule in Spain ended in the year 711 with
the death of Roderick in battle. A main cause of
the ruin of the power of the Goths was rivalry
between the royal families of Chindasuintho, who
died in 652, after ten years of rule, and Wamba,
who was dethroned twenty years later, and died in
a monastery. Witiza, who was sole king in the
year 701, was of the family of Wamba. He put
out the eyes of Theodofred, a younger son of
Chindasuintho, and murdered Favila, another son,
at the instigation of Favila's wife, with whom he
then lived in adultery. Favila's son, Pelayo, he
drove into exile. Theodofred's son was Roderick,
who recovered the throne, so re-establishing the
family of Chindasuintho. He put out Witiza's
eyes, but spared Witiza's brother Orpas because
he was a priest; also Ebba and Sisibert, who were
sons of Witiza by the mother of Pelayo. The sup-
porters of the rival family of Wamba sought aid
from the Moors against Roderick, and the imme-
diate occasion of the call was said to be the violation of Count Julian's daughter. These are events
before the action of Southey's poem. Roderick's
father, Theodofred, whom Witiza had blinded;
King Witiza, whom Roderick had dethroned and
blinded; Favila, the father of Pelayo, and his
adulterous wife, the mother of Pelayo, are all

dead. The persons of the tale are Pelayo, who
checks the Moors at the battle of Covadonga,
and becomes the founder of a monarchy in Spain,
Christian and national, as king of Asturias; and
Leon, with his unfaithful sister Guisla, his wife
Gaudiosa, his son and daughter, Favila—named
after his grandfather—and Hermesind. There are
the great lords, Count Eudon and Count Pedro;
and Count Pedro's son, Alphonso, à heroic youth, to
become twenty years afterwards king of the free and
Christian part of Spain, as Alphonso the Catholic.
Witiza's brother, Orpas, and Witiza's sons, Sisibert
and Ebba, come also into the story; Count Julian,
of course, and Florinda; Roderick's mother Rusilla, and Abdalaziz, Moorish governor of Spain, to
whom Roderick's wife Egilona has attached herself. Urban, Archbishop of Toledo, and the monk
Romano are to be found in the old records, but
Adosinda and Siverian are characters invented by
the poet. Of Southey's invention also is the whole
plot of his beautiful tale of a manly penitence in
Roderick's victory "over the world, his sins, and
his despair." That victory is at the heart of the
heroic tale which ends with the battle that freed part
of Spain from Moorish domination and made Pelayo
the first Spanish king. The English poet's tale of
manly penitence, tried to the quick and with a
saving force for more than Roderick himself, re-
places the old monkish legend of deep penitence
after escape from the battle in which Roderick was
thought to have lost both life and kingdom. The
monk Romano took with him the lost Roderick to
help in saving two very sacred images—one of the
Virgin, one of St. Bartholomew—with which, Roderick carrying the image of the Virgin in his arms,
they journeyed together across mountains and rivers,
for twenty-six days, till they found, by the shore of
Portugal, in the bay of Pederneira, a solitary rock
miraculously rising from the waste sand, and on
the top of it " a little hermitage with a holy crucifix, and no other signs of man save only a plain
tomb, without writing or epitaph to declare whose

it might be." In that hermitage Roderick resolved to end his life. Romano settled in a cave
by the beach more than a mile away, within sight
of the king, and set up in his cave the image of
the Virgin ; but Roderick had in his hermitage the
image of Saint Bartholomew. Roderick and Romano visited each other, and were both much
tempted by the devil. After a year Romano died,
and Roderick buried him. When more time had
passed Roderick was led by a white cloud to
Viseo, where, in the hermitage of St. Michael, he
"ended his days in great penance, no man knowing the manner thereof, neither was there any
other memorial clearer than that, in process of
time, a writing was found upon a certain tomb
in this church with these words: 𝕳𝖎𝖈 𝖗𝖊𝖖𝖚𝖎𝖊𝖘𝖈𝖎𝖙
𝕽𝖚𝖉𝖊𝖗𝖎𝖈𝖚𝖘 𝖚𝖑𝖙𝖎𝖒𝖚𝖘 𝕽𝖊𝖝 𝕲𝖔𝖙𝖇𝖔𝖗𝖚𝖒." There was
also a legend that King Roderick went down into
that tomb alive, together with a two-headed ser-
pent, and so was closed in it. The tomb was
flat, and of a single stone, with barely room for a
man's body. But there was a round hole in the
tomb, and through this, it was said, the snake had
entered.

RODERICK,

THE LAST OF THE GOTHS.

I.

RODERICK AND ROMANO.

LONG had the crimes of Spain cried out to Heaven;
At length the measure of offence was full,
Count Julian called the invaders; not because
Inhuman priests with unoffending blood
Had stained their country; not because a yoke
Of iron servitude oppressed and galled
The children of the soil; a private wrong
Roused the remorseless baron. Mad to wreak
His vengeance for his violated child
On Roderick's head, in evil hour for Spain,
For that unhappy daughter and himself,
Desperate apostate—on the Moors he called;
And like a cloud of locusts, whom the South
Wafts from the plains of wasted Africa,
The Mussulmans upon Iberia's shore
Descend. A countless multitude they came,
Syrian, Moor, Saracen, Greek renegade,
Persian and Copt and Tartar, in one bond
Of erring faith conjoined,—strong in the youth
And heat of zeal,—a dreadful brotherhood,
In whom all turbulent vices were let loose;
While Conscience, with their impious creed accurst
Drunk as with wine, had sanctified to them
All bloody, all abominable things.

Thou, Calpe, saw'st their coming; ancient rock
Renowned, no longer now shalt thou be called
From Gods and heroes of the years of yore,

Kronos, or hundred-handed Briareus,
Bacchus or Hercules; but doomed to bear
The name of thy new conqueror, and thenceforth
To stand his everlasting monument.
Thou saw'st the dark-blue waters flash before
Their ominous way, and whiten round their keels;
Their swarthy myriads darkening o'er thy sands.
There on the beach the misbelievers spread
Their banners, flaunting to the sun and breeze;
Fair shone the sun upon their proud array,
White turbans, glittering armour, shields engrailed
With gold, and scimitars of Syrian steel;
And gently did the breezes, as in sport,
Curl their long flags outrolling, and display
The blazoned scrolls of blasphemy. Too soon
The gales of Spain from that unhappy land
Wafted, as from an open charnel-house,
The taint of death; and that bright sun, from fields
Of slaughter, with the morning dew drew up
Corruption through the infected atmosphere.

Then fell the kingdom of the Goths; their hour
Was come, and Vengeance, long withheld, went
Famine and Pestilence had wasted them,   [loose.
And Treason, like an old and eating sore,
Consumed the bones and sinews of their strength;
And worst of enemies, their sins were armed
Against them. Yet the sceptre from their hands
Passed not away inglorious, nor was shame
Left for their children's lasting heritage;
Eight summer days, from morn till latest eve,
The fatal fight endured, till perfidy
Prevailing to their overthrow, they sunk'
Defeated, not dishonoured. On the banks
Of Chrysus, Roderick's royal car was found,
His battle-horse Orelio, and that helm
Whose horns, amid the thickest of the fray
Eminent, had marked his presence. Did the stream
Receive him with the undistinguished dead,
Christian and Moor, who clogged its course that day?
So thought the conqueror, and from that day forth,
Memorial of his perfect victory,

He bade the river bear the name of Joy.
So thought the Goths ; they said no prayer for him,
For him no service sung, nor mourning made,
But charged their crimes upon his head, and cursed
His memory.
                    Bravely in that eight-days' fight
The King had striven,—for victory first, while hope
Remained, then desperately in search of death.
The arrows passed him by to right and left,
The spear-point pierced him not, the scimitar
Glanced from his helmet.   Is the shield of Heaven,
Wretch that I am, extended over me ?
Cried Roderick ; and he dropt Orelio's reins,
And threw his hands aloft in frantic prayer,—
Death is the only mercy that I crave,
Death soon and short, death and forgetfulness !
Aloud he cried ; but in his inmost heart
There answer'd him a secret voice, that spake
Of righteousness and judgment after death,
And God's redeeming love, which fain would save
The guilty soul alive.   'Twas agony,
And yet 'twas hope ;—a momentary light,
That flashed through utter darkness on the cross
To point salvation, then left all within
Dark as before.   Fear, never felt till then,
Sudden and irresistible as stroke
Of lightning, smote him.   From his horse he dropt,
Whether with human impulse, or by Heaven
Struck down, he knew not ; loosened from his wrist
The sword-chain, and let fall the sword, whose hilt
Clung to his palm a moment ere it fell,
Glued there with Moorish gore.   His royal robe,
His hornéd helmet and enamelled mail,
He cast aside, and taking from the dead
A peasant's garment, in those weeds involved
Stole like a thief in darkness from the field.

        Evening closed round to favour him.   All night
He fled, the sound of battle in his ear
Ringing, and sights of death before his eyes,
With forms more horrible of eager fiends
That seemed to hover round, and gulfs of fire

Opening beneath his feet. At times the groan
Of some poor fugitive, who, bearing with him
His mortal hurt, had fallen beside the way,
Roused him from these dread visions, and he called
In answering groans on his Redeemer's name,
That word the only prayer that passed his lips
Or rose within his heart.   Then would he see
The cross whereon a bleeding Saviour hung,
Who called on him to come and cleanse his soul
In those all-healing streams, which from his wounds,
As from perpetual springs, for ever flowed.
No hart e'er panted for the water-brooks
As Roderick thirsted there to drink and live :
But hell was interposed ; and worse than hell—
Yea to his eyes more dreadful than the fiends
Who flocked like hungry ravens round his head,—
Florinda stood between, and warned him off
With her abhorrent hands,—that agony
Still in her face, which, when the deed was done,
Inflicted on her ravisher the curse
That it invoked from Heaven. . . . Oh what a night
Of waking horrors !   Nor when morning came
Did the realities of light and day
Bring aught of comfort ; wheresoe'er he went
The tidings of defeat had gone before ;
And leaving their defenceless homes to seek
What shelter walls and battlements might yield,
Old men with feeble feet, and tottering babes,
And widows with their infants in their arms,
Hurried along.   Nor royal festival,
Nor sacred pageant, with like multitudes
E'er filled the public way.   All whom the sword
Had spared were here ; bed-rid infirmity
Alone was left behind ; the cripple plied
His crutches, with her child of yesterday
The mother fled, and she whose hour was come
Fell by the road.
            Less dreadful than this view
Of outward suffering which the day disclosed,
Had night and darkness seemed to Roderick's heart,
With all their dread creations.   From the throng
He turned aside, unable to endure

This burthen of the general woe; nor walls,
Nor towers, nor mountain fastnesses he sought,
A firmer hold his spirit yearned to find,
A rock of surer strength.   Unknowing where,
Straight through the wild he hastened on all day,
And with unslackened speed was travelling still
When evening gathered round.   Seven days from
    morn
Till night he travelled thus; the forest oaks,
The fig-grove by the fearful husbandman
Forsaken to the spoiler, and the vines,
Where fox and household dog together now
Fed on the vintage, gave him food; the hand
Of Heaven was on him, and the agony
Which wrought within, supplied a strength beyond
All natural force of man.
                    When the eighth eve
Was come, he found himself on Ana's banks,
Fast by the Caulian Schools.   It was the hour
Of vespers, but no vesper bell was heard,
Nor other sound, than of the passing stream,
Or stork, who flapping with wide wing the air,
Sought her broad nest upon the silent tower.
Brethren and pupils thence alike had fled
To save themselves within the embattled walls
Of neighbouring Merida.   One aged monk
Alone was left behind; he would not leave
The sacred spot beloved, for having served
There from his childhood up to ripe old age
God's holy altar, it became him now,
He thought, before that altar to await
The merciless misbelievers, and lay down
His life, a willing martyr.   So he stayed
When all were gone, and duly fed the lamps,
And kept devotedly the altar drest,
And duly offered up the sacrifice.
Four days and nights he thus had passed alone,
In such high mood of saintly fortitude,
That hope of heaven became a heavenly joy;
And now at evening to the gate he went
If he might spy the Moors,—for it seemed long
To tarry for his crown.

Before the cross
Roderick had thrown himself; his body raised,
Half kneeling, half at length he lay ; his arms
Embraced its foot, and from his lifted face
Tears streaming down bedewed the senseless stone.
He had not wept till now, and at the gush
Of these first tears, it seemed as if his heart,
From a long winter's icy thrall let loose,
Had opened to the genial influences
Of Heaven.   In attitude, but not in act
Of prayer he lay ; an agony of tears
Was all his soul could offer.   When the monk
Beheld him suffering thus, he raised him up,
And took him by the arm, and led him in ;
And there before the altar, in the name
Of Him whose bleeding image there was hung,
Spake comfort, and adjured him in that name
There to lay down the burthen of his sins.
Lo ! said Romano, I am waiting here
The coming of the Moors, that from their hands
My spirit may receive the purple robe
Of martyrdom, and rise to claim its crown.
That God who willeth not the sinner's death
Hath led thee thither.   Threescore years and five,
Even from the hour when I, a five years' child,
Entered the schools, have I continued here
And served the altar : not in all those years
Hath such a contrite and a broken heart
Appeared before me.   O my brother, Heaven
Hath sent thee for thy comfort, and for mine,
That my last earthly act may reconcile
A sinner to his God.
                    Then Roderick knelt
Before the holy man, and strove to speak.
Thou seest, he cried,—thou seest,—but memory
And suffocating thoughts repressed the word,
And shudderings like an ague fit, from head
To foot convulsed him ; till at length, subduing
His nature to the effort, he exclaimed,
Spreading his hands and lifting up his face,
As if resolved in penitence to bear
A human eye upon his shame,—Thou seest

Roderick the Goth! That name would have sufficed
To tell its whole abhorréd history:
He not the less pursued,—the ravisher,
The cause of all this ruin! Having said,
In the same posture motionless he knelt,   [eyes
Arms straightened down, and hands outspread, and
Raised to the monk, like one who from his voice
Awaited life or death.
                        All night the old man
Prayed with his penitent, and ministered
Unto the wounded soul, till he infused
A healing hope of mercy that allayed
Its heat of anguish.   But Romano saw
What strong temptations of despair beset,
And how he needed in this second birth,
Even like a yearling child, a fosterer's care.
Father in heaven, he cried, Thy will be done!
Surely I hoped that I this day should sing
Hosannas at Thy throne; but Thou hast yet
Work for Thy servant here.   He girt his loins,
And from her altar took with reverent hands
Our Lady's image down: In this, quoth he,
We have our guide and guard and comforter,
The best provision for our perilous way.
Fear not but we shall find a resting-place,
The Almighty's hand is on us.
                        They went forth,
They crossed the stream, and when Romano turned
For his last look toward the Caulian towers,
Far off the Moorish standards in the light   .
Of morn were glittering, where the miscreant host
Toward the Lusitanian capital
To lay their siege advanced; the eastern breeze
Bore to the fearful travellers far away
The sound of horn and tambour o'er the plain.
All day they hastened, and when evening fell
Sped toward the setting sun, as if its line
Of glory came from Heaven to point their course.
But feeble were the feet of that old man
For such a weary length of way; and now
Being passed the danger (for in Merida
Sacaru long in resolute defence

Withstood the tide of war), with easier pace
The wanderers journeyed on ; till having crossed
Rich Tagus, and the rapid Zezere,
They from Albardos' hoary height beheld
Pine-forest, fruitful vale, and that fair lake
Where Alcoa, mingled there with Baza's stream,
Rests on its passage to the western sea,
That sea the aim and boundary of their toil.

   The fourth week of their painful pilgrimage
Was full, when they arrived where from the land
A rocky hill, rising with steep ascent,
O'erhung the glittering beach ; there on the top
A little lowly hermitage they found,
And a rude cross, and at its foot a grave,
Bearing no name, nor other monument.
Where better could they rest than here, where faith
And secret penitence and happiest death
Had blessed the spot, and brought good angels
And opened as it were a way to heaven ?   [down,
Behind them was the desert, offering fruit
And water for their need : on either side
The white sand sparkling to the sun ; in front,
Great ocean with its everlasting voice,
As in perpetual jubilee, proclaimed
The wonders of the Almighty, filling thus
The pauses of their fervent orisons.
Where better could the wanderers rest than here?

II.

RODERICK IN SOLITUDE.

TWELVE months they sojourned in their solitude,
And then beneath the burthen of old age
Romano sunk.   No brethren were there here
To spread the sackcloth, and with ashes strew
That penitential bed, and gather round
To sing his requiem, and with prayer and psalm
Assist him in his hour of agony.
He lay on the bare earth, which long had been
His only couch ; beside him Roderick knelt,

Moistened from time to time his blackened lips,
Received a blessing with his latest breath,
Then closed his eyes, and by the nameless grave
Of the fore-tenant of that holy place
Consigned him earth to earth.
                         Two graves are here,
And Roderick transverse at their feet began
To break the third.   In all his intervals
Of prayer, save only when he searched the woods
And filled the water-cruse, he laboured there ;
And when the work was done, and he had laid
Himself at length within its narrow sides
And measured it, he shook his head to think
There was no other business now for him.
Poor wretch, thy bed is ready, he exclaimed,
And would that night were come!—It was a task,
All gloomy as it was, which had beguiled
The sense of solitude ; but now he felt
The burthen of the solitary hours :
The silence of that lonely hermitage
Lay on him like a spell ; and at the voice
Of his own prayers he started half aghast.
Then too as on Romano's grave he sate
And pored upon his own, a natural thought
Arose within him,—well might he have spared
That useless toil ; the sepulchre would be
No.hiding-place for him ; no Christian hands
Were here who should compose his decent corpse
And cover it with earth.   There he might drag
His wretched body at its passing hour,
But there the sea-birds of her heritage
Would rob the worm, or peradventure seize,
Ere death had done its work, their helpless prey.
Even now they did not fear him : when he walked
Beside them on the beach, regardlessly
They saw his coming ; and their whirring wings
Upon the height had sometimes fanned his cheek,
As if, being thus alone, humanity
Had lost its rank, and the prerogative
Of man were done away.
                         For his lost crown
And sceptre never had he felt a thought

Of pain ; repentance had no pangs to spare
For trifles such as these,—the loss of these
Was a cheap penalty ;—that he had fallen
Down to the lowest depth of wretchedness,
His hope and consolation.   But to lose
His human station in the scale of things,—
To see brute nature scorn him, and renounce
Its homage to the human form divine ;—
Had then Almighty vengeance thus revealed
His punishment, and was he fallen indeed
Below fallen man, below redemption's reach,—
Made lower than the beasts, and like the beasts
To perish ?—Such temptations troubled him
By day, and in the visions of the night ;
And even in sleep he struggled with the thought,
And waking with the effort of his prayers,
The dream assailed him still.
                                         A wilder form
Sometimes his poignant penitence assumed,
Starting with force revived from intervals
Of calmer passion, or exhausted rest ;
When floating back upon the tide of thought
Remembrance to a self-excusing strain
Beguiled him, and recalled in long array
The sorrows and the secret impulses
Which to the abyss of wretchedness and guilt
Led their unwary victim.   The evil hour
Returned upon him, when reluctantly
Yielding to worldly counsel his assent,
In wedlock to an ill-assorted mate
He gave his cold unwilling hand : then came
The disappointment of the barren bed,
The hope deceived, the soul dissatisfied,
Home without love, and privacy from which
Delight was banished first, and peace too soon
Departed.   Was it strange that when he met
A heart attuned,—a spirit like his own,
Of lofty pitch, yet in affection mild,
And tender as a youthful mother's joy,—
Oh, was it strange if at such sympathy
The feelings which within his breast repelled
And chilled had shrunk, should open forth like flowers

After cold winds of night, when gentle gales
Restore the genial sun? If all were known,
Would it indeed be not to be forgiven?—
(Thus would he lay the unction to his soul)
If all were truly known, as Heaven knows all,
Heaven that is merciful as well as just,—
A passion slow and mutual in its growth,
Pure as fraternal love, long self-concealed,
And when confessed in silence, long controlled ;
Treacherous occasion, human frailty, fear
Of endless separation, worse than death,—
The purpose and the hope with which the Fiend
Tempted, deceived, and maddened him ;—but then
As at a new temptation would he start,
Shuddering beneath the intolerable shame,
And clench in agony his matted hair ;
While in his soul the perilous thought arose,
How easy 'twere to plunge where yonder waves
Invited him to rest.   Oh for a voice
Of comfort,—for a ray of hope from Heaven !
A hand that from these billows of despair
May reach and snatch him ere he sink engulfed !
At length, as life when it hath lain long time
Opprest beneath some grievous malady,
Seems to rouse up with re-collected strength,
And the sick man doth feel within himself
A second spring ; so Roderick's better mind
Arose to save him.   Lo ! the western sun
Flames o'er the broad Atlantic ; on the verge
Of glowing ocean rests ; retiring then
Draws with it all its rays, and sudden night
Fills the whole cope of heaven.   The penitent
Knelt by Romano's grave, and falling prone,
Claspt with extended arms the funeral mould.
Father ! he cried ; companion ! only friend,
When all beside was lost ! thou too art gone,
And the poor sinner whom from utter death
Thy providential hand preserved, once more
Totters upon the gulf.   I am too weak
For solitude,—too vile a wretch to bear
This everlasting commune with myself.

The Tempter hath assailed me ; my own heart
Is leagued with him ; Despair hath laid the nets
To take my soul, and Memory, like a ghost,
Haunts me, and drives me to the toils.   O saint,
While I was blest with thee, the hermitage
Was my sure haven !   Look upon me still,
For from thy heavenly mansion thou canst see
The suppliant ; look upon thy child in Christ.
Is there no other way for penitence ?
I ask not martyrdom ; for what am I
That I should pray for triumphs, the fit meed
Of a long life of holy works like thine ;
Or how should I presumptuously aspire
To wear the heavenly crown resigned by thee,
For my poor sinful sake ?   Oh point me thou
Some humblest, painfullest, severest path,—
Some new austerity, unheard of yet
In Syrian fields of glory, or the sands
Of holiest Egypt.   Let me bind my brow
With thorns, and barefoot seek Jerusalem,
Tracking the way with blood ; there day by day
Inflict upon this guilty flesh the scourge,
Drink vinegar and gall, and for my bed
Hang with extended limbs upon the cross,
A nightly crucifixion !—anything
Of action, difficulty, bodily pain,
Labour, and outward suffering—anything
But stillness and this dreadful solitude !
Romano ! Father ! let me hear thy voice
In dreams, O sainted Soul ! or from the grave
Speak to thy penitent ; even from the grave
Thine were a voice of comfort.
                              Thus he cried,
Easing the pressure of his burthened heart
With passionate prayer ; thus poured his spirit forth,
Till with the long impetuous effort spent,
His spirit failed, and laying on the grave
His weary head as on a pillow, sleep
Fell on him.   He had prayed to hear a voice
Of consolation, and in dreams a voice
Of consolation came.   Roderick, it said,—
Roderick, my poor, unhappy, sinful child,

Jesus have mercy on thee !—Not if heaven
Had opened, and Romano, visible
In his beatitude, had breathed that prayer ;—
Not if the grave had spoken, had it pierced
So deeply in his soul, nor wrung his heart
With such compunctious visitings, nor given
So quick, so keen a pang.   It was that voice
Which sung his fretful infancy to sleep
So patiently ; which soothed his childish griefs,
Counselled, with anguish and prophetic tears,
His headstrong youth.   And lo ! his mother stood
Before him in the vision ; in those weeds
Which never from the hour when to the grave
She followed her dear lord Theodofred
Rusilla laid aside ; but in her face
A sorrow that bespake a heavier load
At heart, and more unmitigated woe,—
Yea, a more mortal wretchedness than when
Witiza's ruffians and the red-hot brass
Had done their work, and in her arms she held
Her eyeless husband ; wiped away the sweat
Which still his tortures forced from every pore,
Cooled his scorched lids with medicinal herbs,
And prayed the while for patience for herself
And him, and prayed for vengeance too, and found
Best comfort in her curses.   In his dream,
Groaning he knelt before her to beseech
Her blessing, and she raised her hands to lay
A benediction on him.   But those hands
Were chained, and casting a wild look around,
With thrilling voice she cried, Will no one break
These shameful fetters?   Pedro, Theudemir,
Athanagild, where are ye?   Roderick's arm
Is withered ;—chiefs of Spain, but where are ye?
And thou, Pelayo, thou our surest hope,
Dost thou too sleep?—Awake, Pelayo !—up !—
Why tarriest thou, deliverer?   But with that
She broke her bonds, and lo ! her form was changed !
Radiant in arms she stood ! a bloody cross
Gleamed on her breastplate, in her shield displayed
Erect a lion ramped ; her helméd head
Rose like the Berecynthian goddess crowned

With towers, and in her dreadful hand the sword
Red as a firebrand blazed.   Anon the tramp
Of horsemen, and the din of multitudes
Moving to mortal conflict, rang around ;
The battle-song, the clang of sword and shield,
War-cries and tumult, strife and hate and rage,
Blasphemous prayers, confusion, agony,
Rout and pursuit and death ; and over all
The shout of victory—Spain and victory !
Roderick, as the strong vision mastered him,
Rushed to the fight rejoicing : starting then,
As his own effort burst the charm of sleep,
He found himself upon that lonely grave
In moonlight and in silence.   But the dream
Wrought in him still ; for still he felt his heart
Pant, and his withered arm was trembling still ;
And still that voice was in his ear which called
On Jesus for his sake.
               Oh, might he hear
That actual voice ! and if Rusilla lived,—
If shame and anguish for his crimes not yet
Had brought her to her grave,—sure she would bless
Her penitent child, and pour into his heart
Prayers and forgiveness, which, like precious balm,
Would heal the wounded soul.   Nor to herself
Less precious, or less healing, would the voice
That spake forgiveness flow.   She wept her son
For ever lost, cut off with all the weight
Of unrepented sin upon his head,
Sin which had weighed a nation down—what joy
To know that righteous Heaven had in its wrath
Remembered mercy, and she yet might meet
The child whom she had borne, redeemed, in bliss.
The sudden impulse of such thoughts confirmed
That unacknowledged purpose, which till now
Vainly had sought its end.   He girt his loins,
Laid holiest Mary's image in a cleft
Of the rock, where, sheltered from the elements,
It might abide till happier days came on,
From all defilement safe ; poured his last prayer
Upon Romano's grave, and kissed the earth
Which covered his remains, and wept as if
At long leave-taking, then began his way.

III.

ADOSINDA.

'Twas now the earliest morning; soon the sun,
Rising above Albardos, poured his light
Amid the forest, and with ray aslant
Entering its depth, illumed the branchless pines,
Brightened their bark, tinged with a redder hue
Its rusty stains, and cast along the floor
Long lines of shadow, where they rose erect
Like pillars of the temple. With slow foot
Roderick pursued his way; for penitence,
Remorse which gave no respite, and the long
And painful conflict of his troubled soul,
Had worn him down. Now brighter thoughts arose,
And that triumphant vision floated still
Before his sight with all her blazonry,
Her castled helm, and the victorious sword
That flashed like lightning o'er the field of blood.
Sustained by thoughts like these, from morn till eve
He journeyed, and drew near Leyria's walls.
'Twas evensong time, but not a bell was heard;
Instead thereof, on her polluted towers,
Bidding the Moors to their unhallowed prayer,
The cryer stood, and with his sonorous voice
Filled the delicious vale where Lena winds
Through groves and pastoral meads. The sound,
Of turban, girdle, robe, and scimitar, [the sight
And tawny skins, awoke contending thoughts
Of anger, shame, and anguish in the Goth;
The face of human-kind so long unseen
Confused him now, and through the streets he went
With haggéd mien, and countenance like one
Crazed or bewildered. All who met him turned
And wondered as he passed. One stopped him short,
Put alms into his hand, and then desired
In broken Gothic speech, the moon-struck man
To bless him. With a look of vacancy
Roderick received the alms; his wandering eye
Fell on the money, and the fallen king,
Seeing his own royal impress on the piece,

Broke out into a quick convulsive voice,
That seemed like laughter first, but ended soon
In hollow groans suppressed ; the Mussulman
Shrunk at the ghastly sound, and magnified
The name of Allah as he hastened on.
A Christian woman spinning at her door
Beheld him, and, with sudden pity touched,
She laid her spindle by, and running in
Took bread, and following after called him back,
And placing in his passive hands the loaf,
She said, Christ Jesus for His mother's sake
Have mercy on thee !   With a look that seemed
Like idiotcy he heard her, and stood still,
Staring a while ; then bursting into tears
Wept like a child, and thus relieved his heart,
Full even to bursting else with swelling thoughts.
So through the streets, and through the northern gate
Did Roderick, reckless of a resting-place,
With feeble yet with hurried step pursue
His agitated way ; and when he reached
The open fields, and found himself alone
Beneath the starry canopy of heaven,
The sense of solitude, so dreadful late,
Was then repose and comfort.   There he stopped
Beside a little rill, and brake the loaf ;
And shedding o'er that long untasted food
Painful but quiet tears, with grateful soul
He breathed thanksgiving forth, then made his bed
On heath and myrtle.
                            But when he arose
At daybreak and pursued his way, his heart
Felt lightened that the shock of mingling first
Among his fellow-kind was overpast ;
And journeying on, he greeted whom he met
With such short interchange of benison
As each to other gentle travellers give,
Recovering thus the power of social speech
Which he had long disused.   When hunger pressed
He asked for alms : slight supplication served ;
A countenance so pale and woe-begone
Moved all to pity ; and the marks it bore
Of rigorous penance and austerest life,

With something too of majesty that still
Appeared amid the wreck, inspired a sense
Of reverence too. The goat-herd on the hills
Opened his scrip for him ; the babe in arms,
Affrighted at his visage, turned away,
And clinging to the mother's neck in tears
Would yet again look up, and then again
Shrink back, with cry renewed. The bolder imps
Sporting beside the way, at his approach
Brake off their games for wonder, and stood still
In silence ; some among them cried, A saint !
The village matron when she gave him food
Besought his prayers ; and one entreated him
To lay his healing hands upon her child,
For with a sore and hopeless malady
Wasting, it long had lain,—and sure, she said,
He was a man of God.
             Thus travelling on,
He passed the vale where wild Arunca pours
Its wintry torrents ; and the happier site
Of Old Conimbrica, whose ruined towers
Bore record of the fierce Alani's wrath.
Mondego too he crossed, not yet renowned
In poets' amorous lay ; and left behind
The walls at whose foundation pious hands
Of priest and monk and bishop meekly toiled,—
So had the insulting Arian given command.
Those stately palaces and rich domains
Were now the Moor's, and many a weary age
Must Coimbra wear the misbeliever's yoke,
Before Fernando's banner through her gate
Shall pass triumphant, and her hallowed mosque
Behold the hero of Bivar receive
The knighthood which he glorified so oft
In his victorious fields. Oh if the years
To come might then have risen on Roderick's soul,
How had they kindled and consoled his heart !—
What joy might Douro's haven then have given,
Whence Portugal, the faithful and the brave,
Shall take her name illustrious !—what, those walls
Where Mumadona one day will erect
Convent and town and towers, which shall become

B

The cradle of that famous monarchy !
What joy might these prophetic scenes have given,—
What ample vengeance on the Mussulman,
Driven out with foul defeat, and made to feel
In Africa the wrongs he wrought to Spain ;
And still pursued by that relentless sword,
Even to the farthest Orient, where his power
Received its mortal wound.

O years of pride !
In undiscoverable futurity,
Yet unevolved, your destined glories lay ;
And all that Roderick in these fated scenes
Beheld, was grief and wretchedness,—the waste
Of recent war, and that more mournful calm
Of joyless, helpless, hopeless servitude.
'Twas not the ruined walls of church or tower,
Cottage or hall or convent, black with smoke ;
'Twas not the unburied bones, which where the dogs
And crows had strewn them lay amid the field
Bleaching in sun or shower, that wrung his heart
With keenest anguish : 'twas when he beheld
The turbaned traitor show his shameless front
In the open eye of Heaven,—the renegade,
On whose base brutal nature unredeemed
Even black apostacy itself could stamp
No deeper reprobation, at the hour
Assigned fall prostrate ; and unite the names
Of God and the blasphemer,—impious prayer,—
Most impious, when from unbelieving lips
The accursed utterance came. Then Roderick's heart
With indignation burnt, and then he longed
To be a king again, that so, for Spain
Betrayed and his Redeemer thus renounced,
He might inflict due punishment, and make
These wretches feel his wrath. But when he saw
The daughters of the land,—who, as they went
With cheerful step to church, were wont to show
Their innocent faces to all passers' eyes,
Freely, and free from sin as when they looked
In adoration and in praise to heaven,—
Now masked in Moorish mufflers, to the mosque
Holding uncompanied their jealous way,

His spirit seemed at that unhappy sight
To die away within him, and he too
Would fain have died, so death could bring with it
Entire oblivion.
              Rent with thoughts like these,
He reached that city, once the seat renowned
Of Suevi kings, where, in contempt of Rome
Degenerate long, the North's heroic race
Raised first a rival throne ; now from its state
Of proud regality debased and fallen.
Still bounteous nature o'er the lovely vale,
Where like a queen rose Bracara august,
Poured forth her gifts profuse ; perennial springs
Flowed for her habitants, and genial suns,
With kindly showers to bless the happy clime,
Combined in vain their gentle influences :
For patient servitude was there, who bowed
His neck beneath the Moor, and silent grief
That eats into the soul.   The walls and stones
Seemed to reproach their dwellers ; stately piles
Yet undecayed, the mighty monuments
Of Roman pomp, barbaric palaces,
And Gothic halls, where haughty barons late
Gladdened their faithful vassals with the feast
And flowing bowl, alike the spoiler's now.

    Leaving these captive scenes behind, he crossed
Cavado's silver current, and the banks
Of Lima, through whose groves in after years,
Mournful yet sweet, Diogo's amorous lute
Prolonged its tuneful echoes.   But when now
Beyond Arnoya's tributary tide,
He came where Minho rolled its ampler stream
By Auria's ancient walls, fresh horrors met
His startled view ; for prostrate in the dust
Those walls were laid, and towers and temples stood
Tottering in frightful ruins, as the flame
Had left them black and bare ; and through the
    streets,
All with the recent wreck of war bestrewn,
Helmet and turban, scimitar and sword,
Christian and Moor in death promiscuous lay

Each where they fell; and blood-flakes, parched
　　and cracked
Like the dry slime of some receding flood ;
And half-burnt bodies, which allured from far
The wolf and raven, and to impious food
Tempted the houseless dog.
　　　　　　　　　　　　A thrilling pang,
A sweat like death, a sickness of the soul,
Came over Roderick.　Soon they passed away,
And admiration in their stead arose,
Stern joy, and inextinguishable hope,
With wrath, and hate, and sacred vengeance now
Indissolubly linked.　O valiant race,
O people excellently brave, he cried,
True Goths ye fell, and faithful to the last ;
Though overpowered, triumphant, and in death
Unconquered I　Holy be your memory !
Blesséd and glorious now and evermore
Be your heroic names !—Led by the sound,
As thus he cried aloud, a woman came
Towards him from the ruins.　For the love
Of Christ, she said, lend me a little while
Thy charitable help !—Her words, her voice,
Her look, more horror to his heart conveyed
Than all the havoc round : for though she spake
With the calm utterance of despair, in tones
Deep-breathed and low, yet never sweeter voice
Poured forth its hymns in ecstacy to Heaven.
Her hands were bloody, and her garments stained
With blood, her face with blood and dust defiled.
Beauty and youth, and grace and majesty,
Had every charm of form and feature given ;
But now upon her rigid countenance
Severest anguish set a fixedness
Ghastlier than death.
　　　　　　　　　　　She led him through the streets
A little way along, where four low walls,
Heapt rudely from the ruins round, enclosed
A narrow space : and there upon the ground
Four bodies, decently composed, were laid,
Though horrid all with wounds and clotted gore ;
A venerable ancient, by his side

A comely matron, for whose middle age
(If ruthless slaughter had not intervened),
Nature it seemed, and gentle Time, might well
Have many a calm declining year in store ;
The third an arméd warrior, on his breast
An infant, over whom his arms were crossed.
There,—with firm eye and steady countenance,
Unfaltering, she addressed him,—there they lie,
Child, husband, parents,—Adosinda's all !
I could not break the earth with these poor hands,
Nor other tomb provide,—but let that pass !
Auria itself is now but one wide tomb
For all its habitants :—What better grave ?
What worthier monument ?—Oh, cover not
Their blood, thou earth ! and ye, ye blesséd souls
Of heroes and of murdered innocents,
Oh, never let your everlasting cries
Cease round the Eternal Throne, till the Most High
For all these unexampled wrongs hath given
Full, overflowing vengeance !
     While she spake
She raised her lofty hands to Heaven, as if
Calling for justice on the Judgment-seat ;
Then laid them on her eyes, and leaning on,
Bent o'er the open sepulchre.
     But soon
With quiet mien collectedly, like one
Who from intense devotion, and the act
Of ardent prayer, arising, girds himself
For this world's daily business—she arose,
And said to Roderick, Help me now to raise
The covering of the tomb.
     With half-burnt planks,
Which she had gathered for this funeral use,
They roofed the vault, then laying stones above,
They closed it down ; last, rendering all secure,
Stones upon stones they piled, till all appeared
A huge and shapeless heap. Enough, she cried ;
And taking Roderick's hands in both her own,
And wringing them with fervent thankfulness,
May God show mercy to thee, she exclaimed,
When most thou needest mercy ! Who thou art

I know not ; not of Auria,—for of all
Her sons and daughters, save the one who stands
Before thee, not a soul is left alive.
But thou hast rendered to me, in my hour
Of need, the only help which man could give.
What else of consolation may be found
For one so utterly bereft, from Heaven
And from myself must come.   For deem not thou
That I shall sink beneath calamity :
This visitation, like a lightning-stroke,
Hath scathed the fruit and blossom of my youth ;
One hour hath orphaned me, and widowed me,
And made me childless.   In this sepulchre
Lie buried all my earthward hopes and fears,
All human loves and natural charities ;—
All womanly tenderness, all gentle thoughts,
All female weakness too, I bury here,
Yea, all my former nature.   There remain
Revenge and death :—the bitterness of death
Is past, and Heaven already hath vouchsafed
A foretaste of revenge.
      Look here ! she cried,
And drawing back, held forth her bloody hands,—
'Tis Moorish !—In the day of massacre,
A captain of Alcahman's murderous host
Reserved me from the slaughter.   Not because
My rank and station tempted him with thoughts
Of ransom, for amid the general waste
Of ruin all was lost ;—nor yet, be sure,
That pity moved him,—they who from this race
Accurst for pity look, such pity find
As ravenous wolves show the defenceless flock.
My husband at my feet had fallen ; my babe,—
Spare me that thought, O God !—and then—even
Amid the maddening throes of agony [then
Which rent my soul,—when if this solid earth
Had opened and let out the central fire
Before whose all-involving flames wide Heaven
Shall shrivel like a scroll and be consumed,
The universal wreck had been to me
Relief and comfort ;—even then this Moor
Turned on me his libidinous eyes, and bade

His men reserve me safely for an hour
Of dalliance,—me !—me in my agonies !
But when I found for what this miscreant child
Of hell had snatched me from the butchery,
The very horror of that monstrous thought
Saved me from madness ; I was calm at once,—
Yet comforted and reconciled to life :
Hatred became to me the life of life,
Its purpose and its power.
                              The glutted Moors
At length broke up. This hell-dog turned aside
Toward his home ; we travelled fast and far,
Till by a forest edge at eve he pitched
His tents. I washed and ate at his command,
Forcing revolted nature ; I composed
My garments and bound up my scattered hair ;
And when he took my hand, and to his couch
Would fain have drawn me, gently I retired
From that abominable touch, and said,
Forbear to-night, I pray thee, for this day
A widow, as thou seest me, am I made ;
Therefore, according to our law, must watch
And pray to-night. The loathsome villain paused
Ere he assented, then laid down to rest ;
While at the door of the pavilion, I
Knelt on the ground, and bowed my face to earth ;
But when the neighbouring tents had ceased their stir,
The fires were out, and all were fast asleep,
Then I arose. The blessed moon from heaven
Lent me her holy light. I did not pray
For strength, for strength was given me as I drew
The scimitar, and, standing o'er his couch,
Raised it in both my hands with steady aim
And smote his neck. Upward, as from a spring
When newly opened by the husbandman,
The villain's life-blood spouted. Twice I struck
So making vengeance sure : then, praising God,
Retired amid the wood, and measured back
My patient way to Auria, to perform
This duty which thou seest.
                              As thus she spake,
Roderick intently listening had forgot

His crown, his kingdom, his calamities,
His crimes,—so like a spell upon the Goth
Her powerful words prevailed.   With open lips,
And eager ear, and eyes which, while they watched
Her features, caught the spirit that she breathed,
Mute and enrapt he stood, and motionless;
The vision rose before him; and that shout,
Which, like a thunder-peal, victorious Spain
Sent through the welkin, rung within his soul
Its deep prophetic echoes.   On his brow
The pride and power of former majesty
Dawned once again, but changed and purified:
Duty and high heroic purposes
Now hallowed it, and as with inward light
Illumed his meagre countenance austere.

A while in silence Adosinda stood,
Reading his altered visage and the thoughts
Which thus transfigured him. Ay, she exclaimed,
My tale hath moved thee! it might move the dead,
Quicken captivity's dead soul, and rouse
This prostrate country from her mortal trance:
Therefore I live to tell it; and for this
Hath the Lord God Almighty given to me
A spirit not mine own and strength from Heaven;
Dealing with me as in the days of old
With that Bethulian matron when she saved
His people from the spoiler. What remains
But that the life which He hath thus preserved
I consecrate to Him?   Not veiled and vowed
To pass my days in holiness and peace;
Nor yet between sepulchral walls immured,
Alive to penitence alone; my rule
He hath Himself prescribed, and hath infused
A passion in this woman's breast, wherein
All passions and all virtues are combined;
Love, hatred, joy, and anguish, and despair,
And hope, and natural piety, and faith,
Make up the mighty feeling. Call it not
Revenge! thus sanctified and thus sublimed,
'Tis duty, 'tis devotion. Like the grace
Of God, it came and saved me; and in it

Spain must have her salvation.   In thy hands
Here, on the grave of all my family,
I make my vow.
                        She said, and kneeling down,
Placed within Roderick's palms her folded hands.
This life, she cried, I dedicate to God,
Therewith to do Him service in the way
Which He hath shown.   To rouse the land against
This impious, this intolerable yoke,—
To offer up the invader's hateful blood,—
This shall be my employ, my rule and rite,
Observances and sacrifice of faith ;
For this I hold the life which He hath given,
A sacred trust ; for this, when it shall suit
His service, joyfully will lay it down.
So deal with me as I fulfil the pledge,
O Lord my God, my Saviour and my Judge.

 Then rising from the earth, she spread her arms,
And looking round with sweeping eyes exclaimed,
Auria, and Spain, and Heaven receive the vow !

    —⁂—

IV.

THE MONASTERY OF ST. FELIX.

Thus long had Roderick heard her powerful words
In silence, awed before her ; but his heart
Was filled the while with swelling sympathy,
And now with impulse not to be restrained
The feeling overpowered him.   Hear me too,
Auria, and Spain, and Heaven ! he cried ; and thou
Who risest thus above mortality,
Sufferer and patriot, saint and heroine,
The servant and the chosen of the Lord,
For surely such thou art,—receive in me
The first-fruits of thy calling.   Kneeling then,
And placing as he spake his hand in hers,
As thou hast sworn, the royal Goth pursued,
Even so I swear ; my soul hath found at length
Her rest and refuge ; in the invader's blood
She must efface her stains of mortal sin,
And in redeeming this lost land, work out

Redemption for herself.   Herein I place
My penance for the past, my hope to come,
My faith and my good works ; here offer up
All thoughts and passions of mine inmost heart,
My days and night,—this flesh, this blood, this life,
Yea, this whole being do I here devote
For Spain.   Receive the vow, all saints in Heaven,
And prosper its good end !—Clap now your wings,
The Goth with louder utterance as he rose
Exclaimed,—clap now your wings exultingly
Ye ravenous fowl of heaven ; and in your dens
Set up, ye wolves of Spain, a yell of joy ;
For, lo ! a nation hath this day been sworn
To furnish forth your banquet ; for a strife
Hath been commenced, the which from this day forth
Permits no breathing-time, and knows no end
Till in this land the last invader bow
His neck beneath the exterminating sword.

   Said I not rightly? Adosinda cried ;
The will which goads me on is not mine own,
'Tis from on high,—yea, verily of Heaven !
But who art thou who hast professed with me,
My first sworn brother in the appointed rule?
Tell me thy name.
                      Ask anything but that !
The fallen King replied.   My name was lost
When from the Goths the sceptre passed away.
The nation will arise regenerate ;
Strong in her second youth and beautiful,
And like a spirit which hath shaken off
The clog of dull mortality, shall Spain
Arise in glory.   But for my good name
No resurrection is appointed here.
Let it be blotted out on earth : in Heaven
There shall be written with it penitence
And grace and saving faith and such good deeds
Wrought in atonement as my soul this day
Hath sworn to offer up.
                      Then be thy name,
She answered, Maccabee, from this day forth :
For this day art thou born again ; and like

Those brethren of old times, whose holy names
Live in the memory of all noble hearts
For love and admiration, ever young,—
So for our native country, for her hearths
And altars, for her cradles and her graves,
Hast thou thyself devoted.   Let us now
Each to our work.   Among the neighbouring hills,
I to the vassals of my father's house ;
Thou to Visonia.   Tell the Abbot there
What thou hast seen at Auria ; and with him
Take counsel who of all our baronage
Is worthiest to lead on the sons of Spain,
And wear upon his brow the Spanish crown.
Now, brother, fare thee well ! we part in hope,
And we shall meet again, be sure, in joy.

  So saying, Adosinda left the King
Alone amid the ruins.   There he stood,
As when Elisha, on the farther bank
Of Jordan, saw that elder prophet mount
The fiery chariot, and the steeds of fire,
Trampling the whirlwind, bear him up the sky :
Thus gazing after her did Roderick stand ;
And as the immortal Tishbite left behind
His mantle and prophetic power, even so
Had her inspiring presence left infused
The spirit which she breathed.   Gazing he stood,
As at a heavenly visitation there
Vouchsafed in mercy to himself and Spain ;
And when the heroic mourner from his sight
Had passed away, still reverential awe
Held him suspended there and motionless.
Then turning from the ghastly scene of death
Up murmuring Lona, he began toward
The holy Bierzo his obedient way.
Sil's ample stream he crossed, where through the
Of Orras, from that sacred land it bears   [vale
The whole collected waters ; northward then,
Skirting the heights of Aguiar, he reached
That consecrated pile amid the wild,
Which sainted Fructuoso in his zeal
Reared to St. Felix on Visonia's banks.

In commune with a priest of age mature,
Whose thoughtful visage and majestic mien
Bespake authority and weight of care,
Odoar, the venerable Abbot, sate,
When ushering Roderick in, the porter said,
A stranger came from Auria, and required
His private ear.   From Auria? said the old man,
Comest thou from Auria, brother?   I can spare
Thy painful errand then,—we know the worst.

Nay, answered Roderick, but thou hast not heard
My tale.   Where that devoted city lies
In ashes, mid the ruins and the dead
I found a woman, whom the Moors had borne
Captive away ; but she, by Heaven inspired
And her good heart, with her own arm had wrought
Her own deliverance, smiting in his tent
A lustful Moorish miscreant, as of yore
By Judith's holy deed the Assyrian fell.
And that same spirit which had strengthened her
Worked in her still.   Four walls with patient toil
She reared, wherein, as in a sepulchre,
With her own hands she laid her murdered babe,
Her husband and her parents, side by side ;
And when we covered in this shapeless tomb,
There on the grave of all her family,
Did this courageous mourner dedicate
All thoughts and actions of her future life
To her poor country.   For she said, that Heaven
Supporting her, in mercy had vouchsafed
A foretaste of revenge ; that, like the grace
Of God, revenge had saved her ; that in it
Spain must have her salvation ; and henceforth
That passion, thus sublimed and sanctified,
Must be to all the loyal sons of Spain
The pole-star of their faith, their rule and rite,
Observances and worthiest sacrifice.
I took the vow, unworthy as I am,
Her first sworn follower in the appointed rule ;
And then we parted ; she among the hills
To rouse the vassals of her father's house :
I at her bidding hitherward, to ask

Thy counsel, who of our old baronage
Shall place upon his brow the Spanish crown.

The Lady Adosinda? Odoar cried.
Roderick made answer, So she called herself.

Oh, none but she! exclaimed the good old man,
Clasping his hands, which trembled as he spake
In act of pious passion raised to heaven,—
Oh, none but Adosinda!—none but she,—
None but that noble heart, which was the heart
Of Auria while it stood, its life and strength,
More than her father's presence, or the arm
Of her brave husband, valiant as he was.
Hers was the spirit which inspired old age,
Ambitious boyhood, girls in timid youth,
And virgins in the beauty of their spring,
And youthful mothers, doting like herself
With ever-anxious love : She breathed through all
That zeal and that devoted faithfulness,
Which to the invader's threats and promises
Turned a deaf ear alike ; which in the head
And flood of prosperous fortune checked his course,
Repelled him from the walls, and when at length
His overpowering numbers forced their way,
Even in that uttermost extremity
Unyielding, still from street to street, from house
To house, from floor to floor, maintained the fight :
Till by their altars falling, in their doors,
And on their household hearths, and by their beds
And cradles, and their fathers' sepulchres,
This noble army, gloriously revenged,
Embraced their martyrdom.   Heroic souls !
Well have ye done, and righteously discharged
Your arduous part !   Your service is performed,
Your earthly warfare done !   Ye have put on
The purple robe of everlasting peace !
Ye have received your crown !   Ye bear the palm
Before the throne of grace !
                              With that he paused,
Checking the strong emotions of his soul.
Then with a solemn tone addressing him

Who shared his secret thoughts, thou knowest, he
    said,
O Urban, that they have not fallen in vain ;
For by this virtuous sacrifice they thinned
Alcahman's thousands ; and his broken force,
Exhausted by their dear-bought victory,
Turned back from Auria, leaving us to breathe
Among our mountains yet. We lack not here
Good hearts, nor valiant hands. What walls or
Or battlements are like these fastnesses,   [towers
These rocks and glens and everlasting hills?
Give but that Aurian spirit, and the Moors
Will spend their force as idly on these holds,
As round the rocky girdle of the land
The wild Cantabrian billows waste their rage.
Give but that spirit !—Heaven hath given it us,
If Adosinda thus, as from the dead, .
Be granted to our prayers !
                    And who art thou,
Said Urban, who hast taken on thyself
This rule of warlike faith ? Thy countenance
And those poor weeds bespeak a life ere this
Devoted to austere observances.

   Roderick replied, I am a sinful man,
One who in solitude hath long deplored
A life mis-spent ; but never bound by vows,
Till Adosinda taught me where to find
Comfort, and how to work forgiveness out.
When that exalted woman took my vow,
She called me Maccabee ; from this day forth
Be that my earthly name. But tell me now,
Whom shall we rouse to take upon his head
The crown of Spain ? Where are the Gothic chiefs ?
Sacaru, Theudemir, Athanagild,
All who survived that eight days' obstinate fight,
When clogged with bodies Chrysus scarce could force
Its bloody stream along ? Witiza's sons,
Bad offspring of a stock accurst, I know,
Have put the turban on their recreant heads.
Where are your own Cantabrian lords ? I ween,
Eudon, and Pedro, and Pelayo now

Have ceased their rivalry.   If Pelayo live,
His were the worthy heart and rightful hand
To wield the sceptre and the sword of Spain.

Odoar and Urban eyed him while he spake,
As if they wondered whose the tongue might be
Familiar thus with chiefs and thoughts of state.
They scanned his countenance, but not a trace
Betrayed the royal Goth : sunk was that eye
Of sovereignty, and on the emaciate cheek
Had penitence and anguish deeply drawn
Their furrows premature,—forestalling time,
And shedding upon thirty's brow more snows
Than threescore winters in their natural course
Might else have sprinkled.   It seems indeed
That thou hast passed thy days in solitude,
Replied the Abbot, or thou wouldst not ask
Of things so long gone by.   Athanagild
And Theudemir have taken on their necks
The yoke.   Sacaru played a nobler part.
Long within Merida did he withstand
The invader's hot assault ; and when at length,
Hopeless of all relief, he yielded up
The gates, disdaining in his father's land
To breathe the air of bondage, with a few
Found faithful till the last, indignantly
Did he toward the ocean bend his way,
And shaking from his feet the dust of Spain,
Took ship, and hoisted sail through seas unknown
To seek for freedom.   Our Cantabrian chiefs
All have submitted, but the wary Moor
Trusteth not all alike : At his own court
He holds Pelayo, as suspecting most
That calm and manly spirit ; Pedro's son
There too is held as hostage, and secures
His father's faith ; Count Eudon is despised,
And so lives unmolested.   When he pays
His tribute, an uncomfortable thought
May then perhaps disturb him :—or more like
He meditates how profitable 'twere
To be a Moor ; and if apostacy
Were all, and to be unbaptized might serve,—

But I waste breath upon a wretch like this ;
Pelayo is the only hope of Spain,
Only Pelayo.
                        If, as we believe,
Said Urban then, the hand of Heaven is here,
And dreadful though they be, yet for wise end
Of good, these visitations do its work ;
And dimly as our mortal sight may scan
The future, yet methinks my soul descries
How in Pelayo should the purposes
Of Heaven be best accomplished.   All too long,
Here in their own inheritance, the sons
Of Spain have groaned beneath a foreign yoke,
Punic and Roman, Kelt, and Goth, and Greek :
This latter tempest comes to sweep away
All proud distinctions which commingling blood
And time's long course have failed to efface; and now
Perchance it is the will of Fate to rear
Upon the soil of Spain a Spanish throne,
Restoring in Pelayo's native line
The sceptre to the Spaniard.
                        Go thou, then,
And seek Pelayo at the conqueror's court.
Tell him the mountaineers are unsubdued ;
The precious time they needed hath been gained
By Auria's sacrifice, and all they ask
Is him to guide them on.   In Odoar's name
And Urban's, tell him that the hour is come.

   Then pausing for a moment, he pursued :
The rule which thou hast taken on thyself
Toledo ratifies : 'tis meet for Spain,
And as the will divine, to be received,
Observed, and spread abroad.   Come hither thou,
Who for thyself hath chosen the good part ;
Let me lay hands on thee, and consecrate
Thy life unto the Lord.
                        Me ! Roderick cried ;
Me ! sinner that I am !—and while he spake
His withered cheek grew paler, and his limbs
Shook.   As thou goest among the infidels,
Pursued the Primate, many thou wilt find

Fallen from the faith; by weakness some betrayed,
Some led astray by baser hope of gain,
And haply too by ill example led
Of those in whom they trusted. Yet have these
Their lonely hours, when sorrow, or the touch
Of sickness, and that awful power divine
Which hath its dwelling in the heart of man,
Life of his soul, his monitor and judge,
Move them with silent impulse; but they look
For help, and finding none to succour them,
The irrevocable moment passeth by.
Therefore, my brother, in the name of Christ
Thus I lay hands on thee, that in His name
Thou with His gracious promises may'st raise
The fallen, and comfort those that are in need,
And bring salvation to the penitent.
Now, brother, go thy way, the peace of God
Be with thee, and His blessing prosper us!

V.

RODERICK AND SIVERIAN.

BETWEEN St. Felix and the regal seat
Of Abdalazis, ancient Cordoba,
Lay many a long day's journey interposed;
And many a mountain range hath Roderick crossed,
And many a lovely vale, ere he beheld
Where Betis, winding through the unbounded plain
Rolled his majestic waters. There at eve
Entering an inn, he took his humble seat
With other travellers round the crackling hearth,
Where heath and cistus gave their fragrant flame.
That flame no longer, as in other times,
Lit up the countenance of easy mirth   [round
And light discourse: the talk which now went
Was of the grief that pressed on every heart;
Of Spain subdued; the sceptre of the Goths
Broken; their nation and their name effaced;
Slaughter and mourning, which had left no house
Unvisited; and shame, which left its mark
On every Spaniard's face. One who had seen

His sons fall bravely at his side, bewailed
The unhappy chance which, rescuing him from
Left him the last of all his family ;   [death,
Yet he rejoiced to think that none who drew
Their blood from him remained to wear the yoke,
Be at the miscreant's beck, and propagate
A breed of slaves to serve them.   Here sate one
Who told of fair possessions lost, and babes
To goodly fortunes born, of all bereft.
Another for a virgin daughter mourned,
The lewd barbarian's spoil.   A fourth had seen
His only child forsake him in his age,
And for a Moor renounce her hope in Christ.
His was the heaviest grief of all, he said ;
And clenching as he spake his hoary locks,
He cursed King Roderick's soul.
                              Oh curse him not !
Roderick exclaimed, all shuddering as he spake.
Oh, for the love of Jesus, curse him not !
Sufficient is the dreadful load of guilt
That lies upon his miserable soul !
O brother, do not curse that sinful soul,
Which Jesus suffered on the cross to save !

But then an old man who had sate thus long
A silent listener, from his seat arose,
And moving round to Roderick, took his hand ;
Christ bless thee, brother, for that Christian speech,
He said : and shame on me that any tongue
Readier than mine was found to utter it !
His own emotion filled him while he spake,
So that he did not feel how Roderick's hand
Shook like a palsied limb ; and none could see
How, at his well-known voice, the countenance
Of that poor traveller suddenly was changed,
And sunk with deadlier paleness ; for the flame
Was spent, and from behind him, on the wall
High hung, the lamp with feeble glimmering played.

Oh it is ever thus ! the old man pursued,
The crimes and woes of universal Spain
Are charged on him ; and curses which should aim
At living heads, pursue beyond the grave

His poor unhappy soul! As if his sin
Had wrought the fall of our old monarchy!
As if the Mussulmans in their career
Would ne'er have overleapt the gulf which parts
Iberia from the Mauritanian shore,
If Julian had not beckoned them!—Alas!
The evils which drew on our overthrow,
Would soon by other means have wrought their end,
Though Julian's daughter should have lived and died
A virgin vowed and veiled.
                              Touch not on that,
Shrinking with inward shiverings at the thought,
The penitent exclaimed. Oh, if thou lovest
The soul of Roderick, touch not on that deed!
God in His mercy may forgive it him,
But human tongue must never speak his name
Without reproach and utter infamy,
For that abhorréd act. Even thou—but here
Siverian taking up the word, brake off
Unwittingly the incautious speech. Even I,
Quoth he, who nursed him in his father's hall,—
Even I can only for that deed of shame
Offer in agony my secret prayers.
But Spain hath witnessed other crimes as foul:
Have we not seen Favila's shameless wife,
Throned in Witiza's ivory car, parade
Our towns with regal pageantry, and bid
The murderous tyrant in her husband's blood
Dip his adulterous hand? Did we not see
Pelayo, by that bloody king's pursuit,
And that unnatural mother, from the land
With open outcry, like an outlawed thief,
Hunted? And saw ye not Theodofred,
As through the streets I guided his dark steps,
Roll mournfully toward the noon-day sun
His blank and senseless eyeballs? Spain saw this,
And suffered it!—I seek not to excuse
The sin of Roderick. Jesu, who beholds
The burning tears I shed in solitude,
Knows how I plead for him in midnight prayer.
But if, when he victoriously revenged
The wrongs of Chindasuintho's house, his sword

Had not for mercy turned aside its edge,
Oh what a day of glory had there been
Upon the banks of Chrysus!   Curse not him,
Who in that fatal conflict to the last
So valiantly maintained his country's cause ;
But if your sorrow needs must have its vent
In curses, let your imprecations strike
The caitiffs, who, when Roderick's hornéd helm
Rose eminent amid the thickest fight,
Betraying him who spared and trusted them,
Forsook their king, their country, and their God,
And gave the Moor his conquest.
                              Ay! they said,
These were Witiza's hateful progeny ;
And in an evil hour the unhappy King
Had spared the viperous brood.   With that they
How Sisibert and Ebba through the land   [talked
Guided the foe : and Orpas, who had cast
The mitre from his renegado brow,
Went with the armies of the infidels ;
And how in Hispalis, even where his hands
Had ministered so oft the bread of life,
The circumcised apostate did not shame
To show in open day his turbaned head.
The Queen too, Egilona, one exclaimed ;
Was she not married to the enemy,
The Moor, the misbeliever?   What a heart
Were hers, that she could pride and plume herself
To rank among his crowd of concubines,
Having been what she had been !   And who could
How far domestic wrongs and discontent   [say
Had wrought upon the King!—Hereat the old
Raising beneath the knit and curly brow   [man,
His mournful eyes, replied, This I can tell,
That that unquiet spirit and unblest,
Though Roderick never told his sorrows, drove
Rusilla from the palace of her son.
She could not bear to see his generous mind
Wither beneath the unwholesome influence,
And cankering at the core.   And I know well
That oft when she deplored his barren bed,
The thought of Egilona's qualities

Came like a bitter medicine for her grief,
And to the extinction of her husband's line,
Sad consolation, reconciled her heart.

But Roderick, while they communed thus, had
To hear, such painfulest anxiety   [ceased
The sight of that old venerable man
Awoke. A sickening fear came over him:
The hope which led him from his hermitage
Now seemed for ever gone, for well he knew
Nothing but death could break the ties which bound
That faithful servant to his father's house.
She then for whose forgiveness he had yearned,
Who in her blessing would have given and found
The peace of Heaven,—she then was to the grave   ·
Gone down disconsolate at last ; in this
Of all the woes of her unhappy life
Unhappiest, that she did not live to see
God had vouchsafed repentance to her child.
But then a hope arose that yet she lived ;
The weighty cause which led Siverian here
Might draw him from her side ; better to know
The worst than fear it. And with that he bent
Over the embers, and with head half raised
Aslant, and shadowed by his hand, he said,
Where is King Roderick's mother? lives she still?

God hath upheld her, the old man replied ;
She bears this last and heaviest of her griefs,
Not as she bore her husband's wrongs, when hope
And her indignant heart supported her ;
But patiently, like one who finds from Heaven
A comfort which the world can neither give
Nor take away.—Roderick inquired no more ;
He breathed a silent prayer in gratitude,
Then wrapt his cloak around him, and lay down
Where he might weep unseen.
                         When morning came,
Earliest of all the travellers he went forth,
And lingered for Siverian by the way,
Beside a fountain, where the constant fall
Of water its perpetual gurgling made,

To the wayfarer or the musing man
Sweetest of all sweet sounds. The Christian hand,
Whose general charity for man and beast
Built it in better times, had with a cross
Of well-hewn stone crested the pious work,
Which now the misbelievers had cast down,
And broken in the dust it lay defiled.
Roderick beheld it lying at his feet,
And gathering reverently the fragments up,
Placed them within the cistern, and restored
With careful collocation its dear form,—
So might the waters, like a crystal shrine,
Preserve it from pollution. Kneeling then,
O'er the memorial of redeeming love
He bent, and mingled with the fount his tears,
And poured his spirit to the Crucified.

A Moor came by, and seeing him, exclaimed,
Ah, Kaffre! worshipper of wood and stone,
God's curse confound thee! And as Roderick turned
His face, the miscreant spurned him with his foot
Between the eyes. The indignant King arose,
And felled him to the ground. But then the Moor
Drew forth his dagger, rising as he cried,
What, darest thou, thou infidel and slave,
Strike a believer? and he aimed a blow
At Roderick's breast. But Roderick caught his arm,
And closed, and wrenched the dagger from his hold,—
Such timely strength did those emaciate limbs
From indignation draw,—and in his neck
With mortal stroke he drove the avenging steel
Hilt deep. Then, as the thirsty sand drank in
The expiring miscreant's blood, he looked around
In sudden apprehension, lest the Moors
Had seen them; but Siverian was in sight,
The only traveller, and he smote his mule
And hastened up. Ah, brother! said the old man,
Thine is a spirit of the ancient mould!
And would to God a thousand men like thee
Had fought at Roderick's side on that last day
When treason overpowered him! Now, alas!
A manly Gothic heart doth ill accord

With these unhappy times. Come, let us hide
This carrion, while the favouring hour permits.

So saying he alighted. Soon they scooped
Amid loose-lying sand a hasty grave,
And levelled over it the easy soil.
Father, said Roderick, as they journeyed on,
Let this thing be a seal and sacrament
Of truth between us : Wherefore should there be
Concealment between two right Gothic hearts
In evil days like ours? What thou hast seen
Is but the first fruit of the sacrifice,
Which on this injured and polluted soil,
As on a bloody altar, I have sworn
To offer to insulted Heaven for Spain,
Her vengeance and her expiation. This
Was but a hasty act, by sudden wrong
Provoked : but I am bound for Cordoba,
On weighty mission from Visonia sent,
To breathe into Pelayo's ear a voice
Of spirit-stirring power, which like the trump
Of the Archangel, shall awake dead Spain.
The northern mountaineers are unsubdued ;
They call upon Pelayo for their chief ;
Odoar and Urban tell him that the hour
Is come. Thou too, I ween, old man, art charged
With no light errand, or thou wouldst not now
Have left the ruins of thy master's house.

Who art thou? cried Siverian, as he searched
The wan and withered features of the King.
The face is of a stranger, but thy voice
Disturbs me like a dream.
                            Roderick replied,
Thou seest me as I am,—a stranger ; one
Whose fortunes in the general wreck were lost,
His name and lineage utterly extinct,
Himself in mercy spared, surviving all ;—
In mercy, that the bitter cup might heal
A soul diseased. Now, having cast the slough
Of old offences, thou beholdest me
A man new-born ; in second baptism named,
Like those who in Judea bravely raised

Against the heathen's impious tyranny
The banner of Jehovah, Maccabee ;
So call me.   In that name hath Urban laid
His consecrating hands upon my head ;
And in that name have I myself for Spain
Devoted.   Tell me now why thou art sent
To Cordoba ; for sure thou goest not
An idle gazer to the conqueror's court.

Thou judgest well, the old man replied.   I too
Seek the Cantabrian Prince, the hope of Spain,
With other tidings charged, for other end
Designed, yet such as well may work with thine.
My noble mistress sends me to avert
The shame that threats his house.   The renegade
Numacian, he who for the infidels
Oppresses Gegio, insolently woos
His sister.   Moulded in a wicked womb,
The unworthy Guisla hath inherited
Her mother's leprous taint ; and willingly
She to the circumcised and upstart slave,
Disdaining all admonishment, gives ear.
The Lady Gaudiosa sees in this,
With the quick foresight of maternal care,
The impending danger to her husband's house,
Knowing his generous spirit ne'er will brook
The base alliance.   Guisla lewdly sets
His will at nought ; but that vile renegade,
From hatred, and from avarice, and from fear,
Will seek the extinction of Pelayo's line.
This too my venerable mistress sees ;
Wherefore these valiant and high-minded dames
Send me to Cordoba ; that if the Prince
Cannot by timely interdiction stop
The irrevocable act of infamy,
He may at least to his own safety look,
Being timely warned.
                          Thy mistress sojourns then
With Gaudiosa, in Pelayo's hall?
Said Roderick.   'Tis her natural home, rejoined
Siverian ; Chindasuintho's royal race
Have ever shared one lot of weal or woe :

And she who hath beheld her own fair shoot,
The goodly summit of that ancient tree,
Struck by Heaven's bolt, seeks shelter now beneath
The only branch of its majestic stem
That still survives the storm.
                              Thus they pursued
Their journey, each from other gathering store
For thought, with many a silent interval
Of mournful meditation, till they saw
The temples and the towers of Cordoba
Shining majestic in the light of eve.
Before them Betis rolled his glittering stream,
In many a silvery winding traced afar
Amid the ample plain.   Behind the walls
And stately piles which crowned its margin, rich
With olives, and with sunny slope of vines,
And many a lovely hamlet interspersed,
Whose citron bowers were once the abode of peace,
Height above height, receding hills were seen
Imbued with evening hues ; and over all
The summits of the dark sierra rose,
Lifting their heads amid the silent sky.
The traveller who with a heart at ease
Had seen the goodly vision, would have loved
To linger, seeking with insatiate sight
To treasure up its image, deep impressed,
A joy for years to come.   O Cordoba !
Exclaimed the old man, how princely are thy towers,
How fair thy vales, thy hills how beautiful !
The sun who sheds on thee his parting smiles
Sees not in all his wide career a scene
Lovelier, nor more exuberantly blest
By bounteous earth and heaven.   The very gales
Of Eden waft not from the immortal bowers
Odours to sense more exquisite, than these
Which, breathing from thy groves and gardens, now
Recall in me such thoughts of bitterness.
The time has been when happy was their lot
Who had their birthright here ; but happy now
Are they who to thy bosom are gone home,
Because they feel not in their graves the feet
That trample upon Spain.   'Tis well that age

c

Hath made me like a child, that I can weep;
My heart would else have broken, overcharged,
And I, false servant, should lie down to rest
Before my work is done.
                              Hard by their path,
A little way without the walls, there stood
An edifice, whereto, as by a spell,
Siverian's heart was drawn. Brother, quoth he,
'Tis like the urgency of our return
Will brook of no retardment ; and this spot
It were a sin if I should pass, and leave
Unvisited. Beseech you turn with me,
The while I offer up one duteous prayer.

   Roderick made no reply. He had not dared
To turn his face toward those walls ; but now
He followed where the old man led the way.
Lord ! in his heart the silent sufferer said,
Forgive my feeble soul, which would have shrunk
From this,—for what am I that I should put
The bitter cup aside ! O let my shame
And anguish be accepted in Thy sight !

—☙☙—

VI.

RODERICK IN TIMES PAST.

THE mansion whitherward they went, was one
Which in his youth Theodofred had built :
Thither had he brought home in happy hour
His blooming bride ; there fondled on his knee
The lovely boy she bore him. Close beside,
A temple to that saint he reared, who first,
As old tradition tells, proclaimed to Spain
The Gospel-tidings ; and in health and youth,
There mindful of mortality, he saw
His sepulchre prepared. Witiza took
For his adulterous leman and himself
The stately pile : but to that sepulchre,
When from captivity and darkness death
Enlarged him, was Theodofred consigned ;

For that unhappy woman, wasting then
Beneath a mortal malady, at heart
Was smitten, and the tyrant at her prayer
This poor and tardy restitution made.
Soon the repentant sinner followed him ;
And calling on Pelayo ere she died,
For his own wrongs, and for his father's death,
Implored forgiveness of her absent child,—
If it were possible he could forgive
Crimes black as hers, she said. And by the pangs
Of her remorse,—by her last agonies,—
The unutterable horrors of her death,—
And by the blood of Jesus on the cross
For sinners given, did she beseech his prayers
In aid of her most miserable soul.
Thus mingling sudden shrieks with hopeless vows,
And uttering frantically Pelayo's name,
And crying out for mercy in despair,
Here had she made her dreadful end, and here
Her wretched body was deposited.
That presence seemed to desecrate the place :
Thenceforth the usurper shunned it with the heart
Of conscious guilt ; nor could Rusilla bear
These groves and bowers, which, like funereal shades,
Oppressed her with their monumental forms ;
One day of bitter and severe delight,
When Roderick came for vengeance, she endured,
And then for ever left her bridal halls.

Oh, when I last beheld yon princely pile,
Exclaimed Siverian, with what other thoughts
Full, and elate of spirit, did I pass
Its joyous gates ! The weedery which through
The interstices of those neglected courts
Unchecked had flourished long, and seeded there,
Was trampled then and bruised beneath the feet
Of thronging crowds. Here drawn in fair array,
The faithful vassals of my master's house,
Their javelins sparkling to the morning sun,
Spread their triumphant banners ; high-plumed helms
Rose o'er the martial ranks, and prancing steeds
Made answer to the trumpet's stirring voice ;

While yonder towers shook the dull silence off
Which long to their deserted walls had clung,
And with redoubling echoes swelled the shout
That hailed victorious Roderick.   Louder rose
The acclamation, when the dust was seen
Rising beneath his chariot-wheels far off;
But nearer as the youthful hero came,
All sounds of all the multitude were hushed,
And from the thousands and ten thousands here,
Whom Cordoba and Hispalis sent forth,—
Yea, whom all Bætica, all Spain poured out
To greet his triumph,—not a whisper rose
To Heaven, such awe and reverence mastered them,
Such expectation held them motionless.
Conqueror and King he came; but with no joy
Of conquest, and no pride of sovereignty
That day displayed; for at his father's grave
Did Roderick come to offer up his vow
Of vengeance well performed.   Three coal-black
          steeds
Drew on his ivory chariot : by his side,
Still wrapt in mourning for the long-deceased,
Rusilla sate; a deeper paleness blanched
Her faded countenance, but in her eye
The light of her majestic nature shone.
Bound, and expecting at their hands the death
So well deserved, Witiza followed them;
Aghast and trembling, first he gazed around,
Wildly from side to side; then from the face
Of universal execration shrunk,
Hanging his wretched head abased; and poor
Of spirit, with unmanly tears deplored
His fortune, not his crimes.   With bolder front,
Confiding in his priestly character,
Came Orpas next; and then the spurious race
Whom in unhappy hour Favila's wife
Brought forth for Spain.   Oh, mercy ill bestowed,
When Roderick, in compassion for their youth,
And for Pelayo's sake, forebore to crush
The brood of vipers !
                    Err perchance he might,
Replied the Goth, suppressing as he spake

All outward signs of pain, though every word
Went like a dagger to his bleeding heart ;—
But sure, I ween, that error is not placed
Among his sins. Old man, thou mayest regret
The mercy ill deserved, and worse returned,
But not for this wouldst thou reproach the King !

Reproach him? cried Siverian ;—I reproach
My child,—my noble boy,—whom every tongue
Blessed at that hour,—whose love filled every heart
With joy, and every eye with joyful tears !
My brave, my beautiful, my generous boy !
Brave, beautiful, and generous as he was,
Never so brave, so beautiful, so great
As then,—not even on that glorious day,
When on the field of victory, elevate
Amid the thousands who acclaimed him King,
Firm on the shield above their heads upraised,
Erect he stood, and waved his bloody sword.—
Why dost thou shake thy head as if in doubt?
I do not dream, nor fable ! Ten short years
Have scarcely passed away, since all within
The Pyrenean hills, and the three seas
Which girdle Spain, echoed in one response
The acclamation from that field of fight—
Or doth aught ail thee, that thy body quakes
And shudders thus?
                         'Tis but a chill, replied
The King, in passing from the open air
Under the shadow of this thick-set grove.

Oh ! if this scene awoke in thee such thoughts
As swell my bosom here, the old man pursued,
Sunshine, or shade, and all things from without,
Would be alike indifferent. Gracious God,
Only but ten short years,—and all so changed !
Ten little years since in yon court he checked
His fiery steeds. The steeds obeyed his hand,
The whirling wheels stood still, and when he leapt
Upon the pavement, the whole people heard,
In their deep silence, open-eared, the sound.
With slower movement from the ivory seat

Rusilla rose, her arm, as down she stept,
Extended to her son's supporting hand ;
Not for default of firm or agile strength,
But that the feeling of that solemn hour
Subdued her then, and tears bedimmed her sight.
Howbeit when to her husband's grave she came,
On the sepulchral stone she bowed her head
A while ; then rose collectedly, and fixed
Upon the scene her calm and steady eye.
Roderick,—oh, when did valour wear a form
So beautiful, so noble, so august?
Or vengeance, when did it put on before
A character so awful, so divine?
Roderick stood up, and reaching to the tomb
His hands, my hero cried, Theodofred !
Father ! I stand before thee once again,
According to thy prayer, when kneeling down
Between thy knees, I took my last farewell ;
And vowed by all thy sufferings, all thy wrongs,
And by my mother's days and nights of woe,
Her silent anguish, and the grief which then
Even from thee she did not seek to hide,
That if our cruel parting should avail
To save me from the tyrant's jealous guilt,
Surely should my avenging sword fulfil
Whate'er he omened.   Oh that time, I cried,
Would give the strength of manhood to this arm
Already would it find a manly heart
To guide it to its purpose !   And I swore
Never again to see my father's face,
Nor ask my mother's blessing, till I brought,
Dead or in chains, the tyrant to thy feet.
Boy as I was, before all saints in heaven,
And highest God, whose justice slumbereth not,
I made the vow.   According to thy prayer,
In all things, oh my father, is that vow
Performed, alas too well ! for thou didst pray,
While looking up I felt the burning tears
Which from thy sightless sockets streamed, drop
    down,—
That to thy grave, and not thy living feet,
The oppressor might be led.   Behold him there,—

Father! Theodofred! no longer now
In darkness, from thy heavenly seat look down,
And see before thy grave thine enemy
In bonds, awaiting judgment at my hand!

Thus, while the hero spake, Witiza stood
Listening in agony, with open mouth,
And head, half-raised, toward his sentence turned;
His eyelids stiffened and pursed up,—his eyes
Rigid, and wild, and wide; and when the King
Had ceased, amid the silence which ensued,
The dastard's chains were heard, link against link
Clinking. At length upon his knees he fell,
And lifting up his trembling hands, outstretched
In supplication,—Mercy! he exclaimed,—
Chains, dungeons, darkness, — anything but
I did not touch his life.   [death!—
                         Roderick replied,
His hour, whenever it had come, had found
A soul prepared: he lived in peace with Heaven,
And life prolonged for him, was bliss delayed.
But life, in pain and darkness and despair,
For thee, all leprous as thou art with crimes,
Is mercy.—Take him hence, and let him see
The light of day no more!
                         Such Roderick was
When last I saw these courts,—his theatre
Of glory;—such when last I visited
My master's grave!—Ten years have hardly held
Their course,—ten little years,—break, break, old
Oh, why art thou so tough!   [heart—
                    As thus he spake
They reached the church. The door before his hand
Gave way; both blinded with their tears, they went
Straight to the tomb; and there Siverian knelt,
And bowed his face upon the sepulchre,
Weeping aloud; while Roderick, overpowered,
And calling upon earth to cover him,
Threw himself prostrate on his father's grave.

Thus as they lay, an awful voice in tones
Severe addressed them. Who are ye, it said,

That with your passion thus, and on this night,
Disturb my prayers? Starting they rose; there stood
A man before them of majestic form
And stature, clad in sackcloth, bare of foot,
Pale, and in tears, with ashes on his head.

VII.

RODERICK AND PELAYO.

'Twas not in vain that on her absent son,
Pelayo's mother from the bed of death
Called for forgiveness, and in agony
Besought his prayers; all guilty as she was,
Sure he had not been human, if that cry
Had failed to pierce him. When he heard the tale
He blessed the messenger, even while his speech
Was faltering,—while from head to foot he shook
With icy feelings from his inmost heart
Effused. It changed the nature of his woe,
Making the burthen more endurable:
The life-long sorrow that remained, became
A healing and a chastening grief, and brought
His soul, in close communion, nearer Heaven.
For he had been her first-born, and the love
Which at her breast he drew, and from her smiles,
And from her voice of tenderness imbibed,
Gave such unnatural horror to her crimes,
That when the thought came over him, it seemed
As if the milk which with his infant life
Had blended, thrilled like poison through his frame.
It was a woe beyond all reach of hope,
Till with the dreadful tale of her remorse
Faith touched his heart; and ever from that day
Did he for her who bore him, night and morn,
Pour out the anguish of his soul in prayer:
But chiefly as the night returned, which heard
Her last expiring groans of penitence,
Then through the long and painful hours, before
The altar, like a penitent himself,

He kept his vigils ; and when Roderick's sword
Subdued Witiza, and the land was free,
Duly upon her grave he offered up
His yearly sacrifice of agony
And prayer.   This was the night, and he it was
Who now before Siverian and the King
Stood up in sackcloth.
                The old man, from fear
Recovering and from wonder, knew him first.
It is the Prince ! he cried, and bending down
Embraced his knees.   The action and the word
Awakened Roderick ; he shook off the load
Of struggling thoughts, which pressing on his heart,
Held him like one entranced ; yet all untaught
To bend before the face of man, confused
A while he stood, forgetful of his part.
But when Siverian cried, My lord, my lord,
Now God be praised that I have found thee thus,
My lord and Prince, Spain's only hope and mine !
Then Roderick, echoing him, exclaimed, My lord,
And Prince, Pelayo !—and approaching near,
He bent his knee obeisant : but his head
Earthward inclined ; while the old man, looking up
From his low gesture to Pelayo's face,
Wept at beholding him for grief and joy.

    Siverian ! cried the chief,—of whom hath Death
Bereaved me, that thou comest to Cordoba ?—
Children, or wife ?—Or hath the merciless scythe
Of this abhorred and jealous tyranny
Made my house desolate at one wide sweep ?

    They are as thou couldst wish, the old man replied,
Wert thou but lord of thine own house again,
And Spain were Spain once more.   A tale of ill
I bear, but one that touches not the heart
Like what thy fears forbode.   The renegade
Numacian woos thy sister, and she lends
To the vile slave, unworthily, her ear :
The Lady Gaudiosa hath in vain
Warned her of all the evils which await
A union thus accurst : she sets at nought
Her faith, her lineage, and thy certain wrath.

Pelayo hearing him, remained a while
Silent ; then turning to his mother's grave,—
O thou poor dust, hath then the infectious taint
Survived thy dread remorse, that it should run
In Guisla's veins? he cried ;—I should have heard
This shameful sorrow anywhere but here !—
Humble thyself, proud heart ; thou, gracious
Be merciful !—it is the original flaw,—   [Heaven,
And what are we ?—a weak unhappy race,
Born to our sad inheritance of sin
And death !—He smote his forehead as he spake,
And from his head the ashes fell, like snow
Shaken from some dry beech-leaves, when a bird
Lights on the bending spray.   A little while
In silence, rather than in thought, he stood '
Passive beneath the sorrow: turning then,
And what doth Gaudiosa counsel me?
He asked the old man ; for she hath ever been
My wise and faithful counsellor.—He replied,
The Lady Gaudiosa bade me say
She sees the danger which on every part
Besets her husband's house.—Here she had ceased ;
But when my noble mistress gave in charge,
How I should tell thee that in evil times
The bravest counsels ever are the best ;
Then that high-minded lady thus rejoined,
Whatever be my lord's resolve, he knows
I bear a mind prepared.
                              Brave spirits ! cried
Pelayo, worthy to remove all stain
Of weakness from their sex ! I should be less
Than man, if, drawing strength where others find
Their hearts most open to assault of fear,
I quailed at danger.   Never be it said
Of Spain, that in the hour of her distress
Her women were as heroes, but her men
Performed the woman's part.
                              Roderick at that
Looked up, and taking up the word, exclaimed,
O Prince, in better days the pride of Spain,
And prostrate as she lies, her surest hope,
Hear now my tale.   The fire which seemed extinct

Hath risen revigorate : a living spark
From Auria's ashes, by a woman's hand
Preserved and quickened, kindles far and wide
The beacon flame o'er all the Asturian hills.
There hath a vow been offered up, which binds
Us and our children's children to the work
Of holy hatred.   In the name of Spain
That vow hath been pronounced, and registered
Above, to be the bond whereby we stand
For condemnation or acceptance.   Heaven
Received the irrevocable vow, and earth
Must witness its fulfilment ; earth and Heaven
Call upon thee, Pelayo ! Upon thee
The spirits of thy royal ancestors
Look down expectant ; unto thee, from fields
Laid waste, and hamlets burnt, and cities sacked,
The blood of infancy and helpless age
Cries out ; thy native mountains call for thee,
Echoing from all their arméd sons thy name.
And deem not thou that hot impatience goads
Thy countrymen to counsels immature.
Odoar and Urban from Visonia's banks
Send me, their sworn and trusted messenger,
To summon thee, and tell thee in their name
That now the hour is come : For sure it seems,
Thus saith the Primate, Heaven's high will to rear
Upon the soil of Spain a Spanish throne,
Restoring in thy native line, O Prince,
The sceptre to the Spaniard.   Worthy son
Of that most ancient and heroic race,
Which with unweariable endurance still
Hath striven against its mightier enemies,
Roman or Carthaginian, Greek or Goth ;
So often by superior arms oppressed,
More often by superior arts beguiled ;
Yet amid all its sufferings, all the waste
Of sword and fire remorselessly employed,
Unconquered and unconquerable still ;—
Son of that injured and illustrious stock,
Stand forward thou, draw forth the sword of Spain,
Restore them to their rights, too long withheld,
And place upon thy brow the Spanish crown.

When Roderick ceased, the princely mountaineer
Gazed on the passionate orator a while,
With eyes intently fixed, and thoughtful brow;
Then turning to the altar, he let fall
The sackcloth robe, which late with folded arms
Against his heart was pressed; and stretching forth
His hands towards the crucifix, exclaimed,
My God and my Redeemer! where but here,
Before Thy awful presence, in this garb,
With penitential ashes thus bestrewn,
Could I so fitly answer to the call
Of Spain; and for her sake and in Thy name,
Accept the crown of thorns she proffers me!

And where but here, said Roderick in his heart,
Could I so properly, with humbled knee
And willing soul, confirm my forfeiture?—
The action followed on that secret thought:
He knelt, and took Pelayo's hand, and cried,
First of the Spaniards, let me with this kiss
Do homage to thee here, my lord and King!—
With voice unchanged and steady countenance
He spake; but when Siverian followed him,
The old man trembled as his lips pronounced
The faltering vow; and rising he exclaimed,
God grant thee, O my Prince, a better fate
Than thy poor kinsman's, who in happier days
Received thy homage here! Grief choked his speech,
And, bursting into tears, he sobbed aloud.
Tears too adown Pelayo's manly cheek
Rolled silently.   Roderick alone appeared
Unmoved and calm; for now the royal Goth
Had offered his accepted sacrifice,
And therefore in his soul he felt that peace
Which follows painful duty well performed,—
Perfect and heavenly peace,—the peace of God.

VIII.

ALPHONSO.

FAIN would Pelayo have that hour obeyed
The call, commencing his adventurous flight,
As one whose soul impatiently endured
His country's thraldom, and in daily prayer
Imploring her deliverance, cried to Heaven,
How long, O Lord, how long !—But other thoughts
Curbing his spirit, made him yet a while
Sustain the weight of bondage. Him alone,
Of all the Gothic baronage, the Moors
Watched with regard of wary policy,—
Knowing his powerful name, his noble mind,
And how in him the old Iberian blood,
Of royal and remotest ancestry,
From undisputed source flowed undefiled ;
His mother's after-guilt attainting not
The claim legitimate he derived from her,
Her first-born in her time of innocence.
He too of Chindasuintho's regal line
Sole remnant now, drew after him the love
Of all true Goths, uniting in himself
Thus by this double right, the general heart
Of Spain. For this the renegado crew,
Wretches in whom their conscious guilt and fear
Engendered cruellest hatred, still advised
The extinction of Pelayo's house ; but most
The apostate Prelate, in iniquity
Witiza's genuine brother as in blood,
Orpas, pursued his life. He never ceased
With busy zeal, true traitor, to infuse
His deadly rancour in the Moorish chief ;
Their only danger, ever he observed,
Was from Pelayo ; root his lineage out,
The Caliph's empire then would be secure,
And universal Spain, all hope of change
Being lost, receive the Prophet's conquering law.
Then did the arch-villain urge the Moor at once
To cut off future peril, telling him
Death was a trusty keeper. and that none

E'er broke the prison of the grave.   But here
Keen malice overshot its mark: the Moor,
Who from the plunder of their native land
Had bought the recreant crew that joined his arms,
Or cheaplier with their own possessions bribed
Their sordid souls, saw through the flimsy show
Of policy wherewith they sought to cloak
Old enmity, and selfish aims: he scorned
To let their private purposes incline
His counsels, and believing Spain subdued,
Smiled, in the pride of power and victory,
Disdainful at the thought of further strife.
Howbeit he held Pelayo at his court,
And told him that until his countrymen
Submissively should lay their weapons down,
He from his children and paternal hearth
Apart must dwell; nor hope to see again
His native mountains and their vales beloved,
Till all the Asturian and Cantabrian hills
Had bowed before the Caliph; Cordoba
Must be his nightly prison till that hour.
This night, by special favour from the Moor
Asked and vouchsafed, he passed without the walls,
Keeping his yearly vigil; on this night
Therefore the princely Spaniard could not fly,
Being thus in strongest bonds by honour held;
Nor would he by his own escape expose
To stricter bondage, or belike to death,
Count Pedro's son.   The ancient enmity
Of rival houses from Pelayo's heart
Had, like a thing forgotten, passed away;
He pitied child and parent, separated
By the stern mandate of unfeeling power,
And almost with a father's eyes beheld
The boy, his fellow in captivity.
For young Alphonso was in truth an heir
Of nature's largest patrimony; rich
In form and feature, growing strength of limb,
A gentle heart, a soul affectionate,
A joyous spirit filled with generous thoughts,
And genius heightening and ennobling all;
The blossom of all manly virtues made

His boyhood beautiful.   Shield, gracious Heaven,
In this ungenial season, perilous,—
Thus would Pelayo sometimes breathe in prayer
The aspirations of prophetic hope,—
Shield, gracious Heaven, the blooming tree! and let
This goodly promise, for Thy people's sake,
Yield its abundant fruitage.
                          When the Prince,
With hope and fear and grief and shame disturbed,
And sad remembrance, and the shadowy light
Of days before him, thronging as in dreams,
Whose quick succession filled and overpowered
A while the unresisting faculty,
Could in the calm of troubled thoughts subdued
Seek in his heart for counsel, his first care
Was for the boy; how best they might evade
The Moor, and renegade's more watchful eye;
And leaving in some unsuspicious guise
The city, through what unfrequented track
Safeliest pursue with speed their dangerous way.
Consumed in cares like these, the fleeting hours
Went by.   The lamps and tapers now grew pale,
And through the eastern window slanting fell
The roseate ray of morn.   Within those walls
Returning day restored no cheerful sounds
Or joyous motions of awakening life;
But in the stream of light the speckled motes,
As if in mimicry of insect play,
Floated with mazy movement.   Sloping down
Over the altar passed the pillared beam,
And rested on the sinful woman's grave
As if it entered there, a light from Heaven.
So be it! cried Pelayo, even so!
As in a momentary interval,
When thought expelling thought, had left his mind
Open and passive to the influxes
Of outward sense, his vacant eye was there,—
So be it, Heavenly Father, even so!
Thus may Thy vivifying goodness shed
Forgiveness there; for let not Thou the groans
Of dying penitence, nor my bitter prayers
Before Thy mercy-seat, be heard in vain!

And thou, poor soul, who from the dolorous house
Of weeping and of pain, dost look to me
To shorten and assuage thy penal term,
Pardon me that these hours in other thoughts
And other duties than this garb, this night
Enjoin, should thus have passed ! Our mother-land
Exacted of my heart the sacrifice ;
And many a vigil must thy son perform
Henceforth in woods and mountain fastnesses,
And tented fields, outwatching for her sake
The starry host, and ready for the work
Of day, before the sun begins his course.

The noble mountaineer, concluding then
With silent prayer the service of the night,
Went forth.   Without the porch awaiting him
He saw Alphonso, pacing to and fro
With patient step and eye reverted oft.
He, springing forward when he heard the door
Move on its heavy hinges, ran to him,
And welcomed him with smiles of youthful love.
I have been watching yonder moon, quoth he,
How it grew pale and paler as the sun
Scattered the flying shades ; but woe is me,
For on the towers of Cordoba the while
That baleful crescent glittered in the morn,
And with its insolent triumph seemed to mock
The omen I had found.—Last night I dreamt
That thou wert in the field in arms for Spain,
And I was at thy side : the infidels
Beset us round, but we with our good swords
Hewed out a way.   Methought I stabbed a Moor
Who would have slain thee ; but with that I woke
For joy, and wept to find it but a dream.

Thus as he spake a livelier glow o'erspread
His check, and starting tears again suffused
The brightening lustre of his eyes.   The Prince
Regarded him a moment steadfastly,
As if in quick resolve, then looking round
On every side with keen and rapid glance,
Drew him within the church.   Alphonso's heart

Throbbed with a joyful boding as he marked
The calmness of Pelayo's countenance
Kindle with solemn thoughts, expressing now
High purposes of resolute hope.   He gazed
All eagerly to hear what most he wished.
If, said the Prince, thy dream were verified,
And I indeed were in the field in arms
For Spain,—wouldst thou be at Pelayo's side?—
If I should break these bonds, and fly to rear
Our country's banner on our native hills,
Wouldst thou, Alphonso, share my dangerous flight,
Dear boy,—and wilt thou take thy lot with me
For death, or for deliverance?
                              Shall I swear?
Replied the impatient boy ; and laying hand
Upon the altar, on his knee he bent,
Looking towards Pelayo with such joy
Of reverential love, as if a God
Were present to receive the eager vow.
Nay, quoth Pelayo : what hast thou to do
With oaths?—Bright emanation as thou art,
It were a wrong to thy unsullied soul,
A sin to nature, were I to require
Promise or vow from thee !   Enough for me
That thy heart answers to the stirring call.
Alphonso, follow thou in happy faith
Alway the indwelling voice that counsels thee ;
And then let fall the issue as it may,
Shall all thy paths be in the light of Heaven,
The peace of Heaven be with thee in all hours.

How then, exclaimed the boy, shall I dischárge
The burthen of this happiness,—how ease
My overflowing soul !—Oh, gracious God,
Shall I behold my mother's face again,—
My father's hall,—my native hills and vales,
And hear the voices of their streams again,—
And free as I was born amid those scenes
Beloved, maintain my country's freedom there,—
Or, failing in the sacred enterprise,
Die as becomes a Spaniard ?—Saying thus,
He lifted up his hands and eyes toward

The image of the Crucified, and cried,
O Thou who didst with Thy most precious blood
Redeem us, Jesu ! help us while we seek
Earthly redemption from this yoke of shame
And misbelief and death.

            The noble boy
Then rose, and would have knelt again to clasp
Pelayo's knees, and kiss his hand in act
Of homage; but the Prince, preventing this,
Bent over him in fatherly embrace,
And breathed a fervent blessing on his head.

IX.

FLORINDA.

THERE sate a woman like a supplicant,
Muffled and cloaked, before Pelayo's gate,
Awaiting when he should return that morn.
She rose at his approach, and bowed her head,
And, with a low and trembling utterance,
Besought him to vouchsafe her speech within
In privacy.   And when they were alone,
And the doors closed, she knelt and claspt his knees,
Saying, A boon ! a boon !   This night, O Prince,
Hast thou kept vigil for thy mother's soul:
For her soul's sake, and for the soul of him
Whom once, in happier days, of all mankind
Thou heldest for thy chosen bosom friend,
Oh, for the sake of his poor suffering soul,
Refuse me not !

           How should I dare refuse,
Being thus adjured? he answered.   Thy request
Is granted, woman,—be it what it may,
So it be lawful, and within the bounds
Of possible achievement :—aught unfit
Thou wouldst not with these adjurations seek.
But who thou art, I marvel, that dost touch
Upon that string, and ask in Roderick's name !—
She bared her face, and, looking up, replied,

Florinda !—Shrinking then, with both her hands
She hid herself, and bowed her head abased
Upon her knee,—as one who, if the grave
Had oped beneath her, would have thrown herself,
Even like a lover, in the arms of Death.

Pelayo stood confused : he had not seen
Count Julian's daughter since in Roderick's court,
Glittering in beauty and in innocence,
A radiant vision, in her joy she moved ;
More like a poet's dream, or form divine,
Heaven's prototype of perfect womanhood,
So lovely was the presence, than a thing
Of earth and perishable elements.
Now had he seen her in her winding-sheet,
Less painful would that spectacle have proved ;
For peace is with the dead, and piety
Bringeth a patient hope to those who mourn
O'er the departed ; but this altered face,
Bearing its deadly sorrow charactered,
Came to him like a ghost, which in the grave
Could find no rest.   He, taking her cold hand,
Raised her, and would have spoken ; but his tongue
Failed in its office, and could only speak
In undertones compassionate her name.

The voice of pity soothed and melted her ;
And when the Prince bade her be comforted,
Proffering his zealous aid in whatsoe'er
Might please her to appoint, a feeble smile ·
Passed slowly over her pale countenance,
Like moonlight on a marble statue.   Heaven
Requite thee, Prince ! she answered.   All I ask
Is but a quiet resting-place, wherein
A broken heart, in prayer and humble hope,
May wait for its deliverance.   Even this
My most unhappy fate denies me here.
Griefs which are known too widely and too well
I need not now remember.   I could bear
Privation of all Christian ordinances,
The woe which kills hath saved me too, and made
A temple of this ruined tabernacle,

Wherein redeeming God doth not disdain
To let His presence shine.   And I could bear
To see the turban on my father's brow,—
Sorrow beyond all sorrows,—shame of shames,—
Yet to be borne, while I with tears of blood,
And throes of agony, in his behalf
Implore and wrestle with offended Heaven.
This I have borne resigned : but other ills
And worse assail me now ; the which to bear,
If to avoid be possible, would draw
Damnation down.   Orpas, the perjured priest,
The apostate Orpas, claims me for his bride.
Obdurate as he is, the wretch profanes
My sacred woe, and woos me to his bed,
The thing I am,—the living death thou seest !

   Miscreant ! exclaimed Pelayo.   Might I meet
That renegado, sword to scimitar,
In open field, never did man approach
The altar for the sacrifice in faith
More sure, than I should hew the villain down !
But how should Julian favour his demand ?—
Julian, who hath so passionately loved
His child, so dreadfully revenged her wrongs !

   Count Julian, she replied, hath none but me,
And it hath, therefore, been his heart's desire
To see his ancient line by me preserved.
This was their covenant when in fatal hour
For Spain, and for themselves, in traitorous bond
Of union they combined.   My father, stung
To madness, only thought of how to make
His vengeance sure ; the prelate, calm and cool,
When he renounced his outward faith in Christ,
Indulged at once his hatred of the King,
His inbred wickedness, and a haughty hope,
Versed as he was in treasons, to direct
The invaders by his secret policy,
And at their head, aided by Julian's power,
Reign as a Moor upon that throne to which
The priestly order else had barred his way.
The African hath conquered for himself ;

But Orpas coveteth Count Julian's lands,
And claims to have the covenant performed.
Friendless, and worse than fatherless, I come
To thee for succour. Send me secretly,—
For well I know all faithful hearts must be
At thy devotion,—with a trusty guide
To guard me on the way, that I may reach
Some Christian land, where Christian rites are free,
And there discharge a vow, alas! too long,
Too fatally delayed. Aid me in this
For Roderick's sake, Pelayo! and thy name
Shall be remembered in my latest prayer.

  Be comforted! the Prince replied ; but when
He spake of comfort, twice did he break off
The idle words, feeling that earth had none
For grief so irremediable as hers.
At length he took her hand, and pressing it,
And forcing through involuntary tears
A mournful smile affectionate, he said,
Say not that thou art friendless while I live!
Thou couldst not to a readier ear have told
Thy sorrows, nor have asked in fitter hour
What for my country's honour, for my rank,
My faith, and sacred knighthood, I am bound
In duty to perform ; which not to do
Would show me undeserving of the names
Of Goth, Prince, Christian, even of man. This day,
Lady, prepare to take thy lot with me,
And soon as evening closes meet me here.
Duties bring blessings with them, and I hold
Thy coming for a happy augury,
In this most awful crisis of my fate.

X.

RODERICK AND FLORINDA.

WITH sword and breastplate, under rustic weeds
Concealed, at dusk Pelayo passed the gate,
Florinda following near, disguised alike.

Two peasants on their mules they seemed, at eve
Returning from the town. Not distant far,
Alphonso by the appointed orange-grove,
With anxious eye and agitated heart,
Watched for the Prince's coming. Eagerly
At every footfall through the gloom he strained
His sight, nor did he recognise him when
The chieftain thus accompanied drew nigh ;
And when the expected signal called him on,
Doubting this female presence, half in fear
Obeyed the call. Pelayo too perceived
The boy was not alone ; he not for that
Delayed the summons, but lest need should be,
Laying hand upon his sword, toward him bent
In act soliciting speech, and low of voice
Inquired if friend or foe. Forgive me, cried
Alphonso, that I did not tell thee this,
Full as I was of happiness, before.
'Tis Hoya, servant of my father's house,
Unto whose dutiful care and love, when sent
To this vile bondage, I was given in charge.
How could I look upon my father's face
If I had in my joy deserted him,
Who was to me found faithful? Right ! replied
The Prince ; and viewing him with silent joy,
Blesséd the mother, in his heart he said,
Who gave thee birth ! but sure of womankind
Most blesséd she whose hand her happy stars
Shall link with thine ! and with that thought the form
Of Hermesind, his daughter, to his soul
Came in her beauty.
                         Soon by devious tracks
They turned aside. The favouring moon arose,
To guide them on their flight through upland paths
Remote from frequentage, and dales retired,
Forest and mountain glen. Before their feet
The fire-flies, swarming in the woodland shade,
Sprung up like sparks, and twinkled round their way ;
The timorous blackbird, starting at their step,
Fled from the thicket with shrill note of fear ;
And far below them in the peopled dell,
When all the soothing sounds of eve had ceased,

The distant watch-dog's voice at times was heard,
Answering the nearer wolf.   All through the night
Among the hills they travelled silently;
Till when the stars were setting, at what hour
The breath of heaven is coldest, they beheld
Within a lonely grove the expected fire,
Where Roderick and his comrade anxiously
Looked for the appointed meeting.   Halting there,
They from the burthen and the bit relieved
Their patient bearers, and around the fire
Partook of needful food and grateful rest.

Bright rose the flame replenished ; it illumed
The cork-tree's furrowed rind, its rifts and swells
And redder scars,—and where its aged boughs
O'erbowered the travellers, cast upon the leaves
A floating, grey, unrealising gleam.
Alphonso, light of heart, upon the heath
Lay carelessly dispread, in happy dreams
Of home ; his faithful Hoya slept beside.
Years and fatigue to old Siverian brought
Easy oblivion ; and the Prince himself,
Yielding to weary nature's gentle will,
Forgot his cares a while.   Florinda sate
Beholding Roderick with fixed eyes intent,
Yet unregardant of the countenance
Whereon they dwelt ; in other thoughts absorbed,
Collecting fortitude for what she yearned,
Yet trembled to perform.   Her steady look
Disturbed the Goth, albeit he little weened
What agony awaited him that hour.
Her face, well nigh as changed as his, was now
Half-hidden, and the lustre of her eye
Extinct ; nor did her voice awaken in him
One startling recollection when she spake,
So altered were its tones.
                         Father, she said,
All thankful as I am to leave behind
The unhappy walls of Cordoba, not less
Of consolation doth my heart receive
At sight of one to whom I may disclose
The sins which trouble me, and at his feet

Lay down repentantly, in Jesu's name,
The burthen of my spirit. In His name
Hear me, and pour into a wounded soul
The balm of pious counsel.—Saying thus,
She drew toward the minister ordained,
And kneeling by him, Father, dost thou know
The wretch who kneels beside thee? she inquired,
He answered, Surely we are each to each
Equally unknown.
                 Then said she, Here thou seest
One who is known too fatally for all,—
The daughter of Count Julian.—Well it was
For Roderick that no eye beheld him now;
From head to foot a sharper pang than death
Thrilled him; his heart, as at a mortal stroke,
Ceased from its functions: his breath failed, and
     when
The power of life recovering set its springs
Again in action, cold and clammy sweat
Starting at every pore suffused his frame.
Their presence helped him to subdue himself;
For else, had none been nigh, he would have fallen
Before Florinda prostrate on the earth,
And in that mutual agony belike
Both souls had taken flight. She marked him not,
For having told her name, she bowed her head,
Breathing a short and silent prayer to Heaven,
While, as a penitent, she wrought herself
To open to his eye her hidden wound.

    Father, at length she said, all tongues amid
This general ruin shed their bitterness
On Roderick, load his memory with reproach,
And with their curses persecute his soul.—
Why shouldst thou tell me this? exclaimed the Goth,
From his cold forehead wiping as he spake
The death-like moisture;—Why of Roderick's guilt
Tell me? Or thinkest thou I know it not?
Alas! who hath not heard the hideous tale
Of Roderick's shame. Babes learn it from their
And children, by their mothers unreproved, [nurses,
Link their first execrations to his name.

Oh, it hath caught a taint of infamy,
That, like Iscariot's, through all time shall last,
Reeking and fresh for ever !
                              There ! she cried,
Drawing her body backward where she knelt,
And stretching forth her arms with head upraised,—
There ! it pursues me still !—I came to thee
Father, for comfort; and thou heapest fire
Upon my head. But hear me patiently,
And let me undeceive thee ; self-abased,
Not to arraign another, do I come ;—
I come a self-accuser, self-condemned
To take upon myself the pain deserved ;
For I have drank the cup of bitterness,
And having drank therein of heavenly grace,
I must not put away the cup of shame.

Thus as she spake she faltered at the close,
And in that dying fall her voice sent forth
Somewhat of its original sweetness. Thou !—
Thou self-abased ! exclaimed the astonished King—
Thou self-condemned !—The cup of shame for thee!
Thee—thee, Florinda !—But the very excess
Of passion checked his speech, restraining thus
From further transport, which had haply else
Mastered him ; and he sate like one entranced,
Gazing upon that countenance so fallen,
So changed : her face, raised from its muffler now
Was turned toward him, and the firelight shone
Full on its mortal paleness ; but the shade
Concealed the King.
                      She roused him from the spell
Which held him like a statue motionless.
Thou too, quoth she, dost join the general curse
Like one who when he sees a felon's grave,
Casting a stone there as he passes by,
Adds to the heap of shame. Oh, what are we
Frail creatures as we are, that we should sit
In judgment man on man ! and what were we,
If the All-merciful should mete to us
With the same rigorous measure wherewithal
Sinner to sinner metes ! But God beholds

D

The secrets of the heart,—therefore His name
Is Merciful. Servant of God, see thou
The hidden things of mine, and judge thou then
In charity thy brother who hath fallen.—
Nay, hear me to the end! I loved the King,—
Tenderly, passionately, madly loved him.
Sinful it was to love a child of earth
With such entire devotion as I loved
Roderick, the heroic Prince, the glorious Goth!
And yet methought this was its only crime,
The imaginative passion seemed so pure:
Quiet and calm, like duty, hope nor fear
Disturbed the deep contentment of that love;
He was the sunshine of my soul, and like
A flower, I lived and flourished in his light.
Oh, bear not with me thus impatiently!
No tale of weakness this, that in the act
Of penitence, indulgent to itself,
With garrulous palliation half repeats
The sin it ill repents. I will be brief,
And shrink not from confessing how the love
Which thus began in innocence, betrayed
My unsuspecting heart; nor me alone,
But him, before whom, shining as he shone
With whatsoe'er is noble, whatsoe'er
Is lovely, whatsoever good and great,
I was as dust and ashes—him, alas!
This glorious being, this exalted Prince,
Even him, with all his royalty of soul,
Did this ill-omened, this accurséd love,
To his most lamentable fall betray
And utter ruin. Thus it was: The King,
By counsels of cold statesmen ill-advised,
To an unworthy mate had bound himself
In politic wedlock. Wherefore should I tell
How Nature upon Egilona's form,
Profuse of beauty, lavishing her gifts,
Left, like a statue from the graver's hands,
Deformity and hollowness beneath
The rich external? For the love of pomp
And emptiest vanity, hath she not incurred
The grief and wonder of good men, the gibes

Of vulgar ribaldry, the reproach of all ;
Profaning the most holy sacrament
Of marriage, to become chief of the wives
Of Abdalaziz, of the infidel,
The Moor, the tyrant-enemy of Spain !
All know her now ; but they alone who knew
What Roderick was can judge his wretchedness,
To that light spirit and unfeeling heart
In hopeless bondage bound.   No children rose
From this unhappy union, towards whom
The springs of love within his soul confined
Might flow in joy and fulness ; nor was he
One, like Witiza, of the vulgar crew,
Who in promiscuous appetite can find
All their vile nature seeks.   Alas for man !
Exuberant health diseases him, frail worm !
And the slight bias of untoward chance
Makes his best virtue from the even line,
With fatal declination, swerve aside.
Ay, thou mayest groan for poor mortality—
Well, father, mayest thou groan !
                              My evil fate
Made me an inmate of the royal house,
And Roderick found in me, if not a heart
Like his,—for who was like the heroic Goth ?—
One which at least felt his surpassing worth,
And loved him for himself.—A little yet
Bear with me, reverend father, for I touch
Upon the point, and this long prologue goes,
As justice bids, to palliate his offence,
Not mine.   The passion, which I fondly thought
Such as fond sisters for a brother feel,
Grew day by day, and strengthened in its growth,
Till the beloved presence had become
Needful as food or necessary sleep,
My hope, light, sunshine, life, and everything.
Thus lapt in dreams of bliss, I might have lived
Contented with this pure idolatry,
Had he been happy : but I saw and knew
The inward discontent and household griefs
Which he subdued in silence ; and alas !
Pity with admiration mingling then,

Alloyed and lowered and humanised my love,
Till to the level of my lowliness
It brought him down ; and in this treacherous heart
Too often the repining thought arose,
That if Florinda had been Roderick's queen,
Then might domestic peace and happiness
Have blessed his home and crowned our wedded
Too often did that sinful thought recur,   [loves.
Too feebly the temptation was repelled.

   See, father, I have probed my inmost soul ;
Have searched to its remotest source the sin ;
And tracing it through all its specious forms
Of fair disguisement, I present it now,
Even as it lies before the eye of God,
Bare and exposed, convicted and condemned.
One eve, as in the bowers which overhang
The glen where Tagus rolls between his rocks
I roamed alone, alone I met the King.
His countenance was troubled, and his speech
Like that of one whose tongue to light discourse
At fits constrained, betrays a heart disturbed :
I too, albeit unconscious of his thoughts,
With anxious looks revealed what wandering words
In vain essayed to hide.   A little while
Did this oppressive intercourse endure,
Till our eyes met in silence, each to each
Telling their mutual tale, then consciously
Together fell abashed.   He took my hand
And said, Florinda, would that thou and I
Earlier had met ! oh, what a blissful lot
Had then been mine, who might have found in thee
The sweet companion and the friend endeared,
A fruitful wife and crown of earthly joys !
Thou too shouldst then have been of womankind
Happiest, as now the loveliest.—And with that,
First giving way to passion first disclosed,
He pressed upon my lips a guilty kiss—
Alas ! more guiltily received than given.
Passive and yielding, and yet self-reproached,
Trembling I stood, upheld in his embrace ;
When coming steps were heard, and Roderick said,

Meet me to-morrow, I beseech thee, here,
Queen of my heart! Oh, meet me here again,
My own Florinda, meet me here again!—
Tongue, eye, and pressure of the impassioned hand
Solicited and urged the ardent suit,
And from my hesitating hurried lips
The word of promise fatally was drawn.
O Roderick, Roderick! hadst thou told me all
Thy purpose at that hour, from what a world
Of woe had thou and I—The bitterness
Of that reflection overcame her then,
And choked her speech.   But Roderick sate the
     while
Covering his face with both his hands close-prest,
His head bowed down, his spirit to such point
Of sufferance knit, as one who patiently
Awaits the uplifted sword.
                    Till now, said she,
Resuming her confession, I had lived,
If not in innocence, yet self-deceived,
And of my perilous and sinful state
Unconscious.   But this fatal hour revealed
To my awakening soul her guilt and shame;
And in those agonies with which remorse,
Wrestling with weakness and with cherished sin,
Doth triumph o'er the lacerated heart,
That night—that miserable night—I vowed,
A virgin dedicate, to pass my life
Immured; and, likè redeemèd Magdalen,
Or that Egyptian penitent, whose tears
Fretted the rock, and moistened round her cave
The thirsty desert, so to mourn my fall.
The struggle ending thus, the victory
Thus, as I thought, accomplished, I believed
My soul was calm, and that the peace of Heaven
Descended to accept and bless my vow,
And in this faith, prepared to consummate
The sacrifice, I went to meet the King.
See, father, what a snare had Satan laid!
For Roderick came to tell me that the Church
From his unfruitful bed would set him free,
And I should be his queen.

                  O let me close
The dreadful tale ! I told him of my vow ;
And from sincere and scrupulous piety,
But more, I fear me, in that desperate mood
Of obstinate will perverse, the which, with pride
And shame and self-reproach, doth sometimes make
A woman's tongue, her own worst enemy,
Run counter to her dearest heart's desire,—
In that unhappy mood did I resist
All his most earnest prayers to let the power
Of holy Church, never more rightfully
Invoked, he said, than now in our behalf,
Release us from our fatal bonds. He urged
With kindling warmth his suit, like one whose life
Hung on the issue ; I dissembled not
My cruel self-reproaches, nor my grief,
Yet desperately maintained the rash resolve ;
Till in the passionate argument he grew
Incensed, inflamed, and maddened or possessed,—
For hell too surely at that hour prevailed,
And with such subtile toils enveloped him,
That even in the extremity of guilt
No guilt he purported, but rather meant
An amplest recompense of life-long love
For transitory wrong, which fate perverse,
Thus madly he deceived himself, compelled,
And therefore stern necessity excused.
Here, then, O father, at thy feet I own
Myself the guiltier ; for full well I knew
These were his thoughts, but vengeance mastered me,
And in my agony I cursed the man
Whom I loved best.
                 Dost thou recall that curse ?
Cried Roderick, in a deep and inward voice,
Still with his head depressed, and covering still
His countenance. Recall it ? she exclaimed ;
Father, I come to thee because I gave
The reins to wrath too long,—because I wrought
His ruin, death, and infamy.—O God,
Forgive the wicked vengeance thus indulged,
As I forgive the King !—But teach me thou
What reparation more than tears and prayers

May now be made ;—how shall I vindicate
His injured name, and take upon myself——
Daughter of Julian, firmly he replied,
Speak not of that, I charge thee ! On his fame
The Ethiop dye, fixed ineffaceably,
For ever will abide ; so it must be,
So should be : 'tis his rightful punishment ;
And if to the full measure of his sin
The punishment hath fallen, the more our hope
That through the blood of Jesus he may find
That sin forgiven him.
                        Pausing then, he raised
His hand, and pointed where Siverian lay
Stretched on the heath. To that old man, said he,
And to the mother of the unhappy Goth,
Tell, if it please thee,—not what thou hast poured
Into my secret ear, but that the child
For whom they mourn with anguish unallayed,
Sinned not from vicious will, or heart corrupt,
But fell by fatal circumstance betrayed,
And if in charity to them thou sayest
Something to palliate, something to excuse
An act of sudden frenzy when the fiend
O'ercame him, thou wilt do for Roderick
All he could ask thee, all that can be done
On earth, and all his spirit could endure.

    Venturing towards her an imploring look,
Wilt thou join with me for his soul in prayer?
He said, and trembled as he spake. That voice
Of sympathy was like Heaven's influence,
Wounding at once and comforting the soul.
O father, Christ requite thee ! she exclaimed ;
Thou hast set free the springs which withering
    griefs
Have closed too long. Forgive me, for I thought
Thou wert a rigid and unpitying judge ;
One whose stern virtue, feeling in itself
No flaw of frailty, heard impatiently
Of weakness and of guilt. I wronged thee, father!—
With that she took his hand, and kissing it,
Bathed it with tears. Then in a firmer speech,

For Roderick, for Count Julian and myself,
Three wretchedest of all the human race,
Who have destroyed each other and ourselves,
Mutually wronged and wronging, let us pray !

XI.

COUNT PEDRO'S CASTLE.

TWELVE weary days with unremitting speed,
Shunning frequented tracks, the travellers
Pursued their way ; the mountain path they chose,
The forest or the lonely heath wide-spread,
Where cistus shrubs sole seen exhaled at noon
Their fine balsamic odour all around,
Strewed with their blossoms, frail as beautiful,
The thirsty soil at eve ; and when the sun
Relumed the gladdened earth, opening anew
Their stores exuberant, prodigal as frail,
Whitened again the wilderness.   They left
The dark sierra's skirts behind, and crossed
The wilds where Ana in her native hills
Collects her sister springs, and hurries on
Her course melodious amid loveliest glens,
With forest and with fruitage overbowered.
These scenes profusely blest by Heaven they left,
Where o'er the hazel and the quince the vine
Wide-mantling spreads : and clinging round the
        cork
And ilex, hangs amid their dusky leaves
Garlands of brightest hue, with reddening fruit
Pendent, or clusters cool of glassy green.
So holding on o'er mountain and o'er vale,
Tagus they crossed where midland on his way
The king of rivers rolls his stately stream ;
And rude Alverches' wide and stony bed,
And Duero distant far, and many a stream
And many a field obscure, in future war
For bloody theatre of famous deeds
Foredoomed : and deserts where in years to come

Shall populous towns arise, and crested towers
And stately temples rear their heads on high.

Cautious with course circuitous they shunned
The embattled city, which in eldest time
Thrice-greatest Hermes built, so fables say,
Now subjugate, but fated to behold
Ere long the heroic Prince (who passing now
Unknown and silently the dangerous track,
Turns thither his regardant eye) come down
Victorious from the heights, and bear abroad
Her bannered Lion, symbol to the Moor
Of rout and death through many an age of blood.
Lo, there the Asturian hills !   Far in the west,
Huge Rabanal and Foncebadon huge,
Pre-eminent their giant bulk display,
Darkening with earliest shade the distant vales
Of Leon, and with evening premature.
Far in Cantabria eastward, the long line
Extends beyond the reach of eagle's eye,
When buoyant in mid-heaven the bird of Jove
Soars at his loftiest pitch.   In the north, before
The travellers the Erbasian mountains rise,
Bounding the land beloved, their native land.

How then, Alphonso, did thy eager soul
Chide the slow hours and painful way, which seemed
Lengthening to grow before their lagging pace !
Youth of heroic thought and high desire,
'T is not the spur of lofty enterprise
That with unequal throbbing hurries now
The unquiet heart, now makes it sink dismayed ;
'T is not impatient joy which thus disturbs
In that young breast the healthful spring of life ;
Joy and ambition have forsaken him,
His soul is sick with hope.   So near his home,
So near his mother's arms ;—alas ! perchance
The longed-for meeting may be yet far off
As earth from heaven.   Sorrow in these long months
Of separation may have laid her low ;
Or what if at his flight the bloody Moor
Hath sent his ministers of slaughter forth,

And he himself should thus have brought the sword
Upon his father's head?—Sure Hoya too
The same dark presage feels, the fearful boy
Said in himself; or wherefore is his brow
Thus overcast with heaviness, and why
Looks he thus anxiously in silence round?

    Just then that faithful servant raised his hand,
And turning to Alphonso with a smile,
He pointed where Count Pedro's towers far off
Peered in the dell below; faint was the smile,
And while it sate upon his lips, his eye
Retained its troubled speculation still.
For long had he looked wistfully in vain,
Seeking where far or near he might espy
From whom to learn if time or chance had wrought
Change in his master's house: but on the hills
Nor goat-herd could he see, nor traveller,
Nor huntsman early at his sports afield,
Nor angler following up the mountain glen
His lonely pastime; neither could he hear
Carol, or pipe, or shout of shepherd's boy,
Nor woodman's axe, for not a human sound
Disturbed the silence of the solitude.

    Is it the spoiler's work? At yonder door
Behold the favourite kidling bleats unheard;
The next stands open, and the sparrows there
Boldly pass in and out. Thither he turned
To seek what indications were within;
The chestnut-bread was on the shelf, the churn,
As if in haste forsaken, full and fresh;
The recent fire had mouldered on the hearth;
And broken cobwebs marked the whiter space
Where from the wall the buckler and the sword
Had late been taken down. Wonder at first
Had mitigated fear, but Hoya now
Returned to tell the symbols of good hope,
And they pricked forward joyfully. Ere long,
Perceptible above the ceaseless sound
Of yonder stream, a voice of multitudes,
As if in loud acclaim, was heard far off;

And nearer as they drew, distincter shouts
Came from the dell, and at Count Pedro's gate
The human swarm were seen,—a motley group, ·
Maids, mothers, helpless infancy, weak age,
And wondering children and tumultuous boys,
Hot youth and resolute manhood gathered there,
In uproar all.   Anon the moving mass
Falls in half-circle back, a general cry
Bursts forth, exultant arms are lifted up
And caps are thrown aloft, as through the gate
Count Pedro's banner came.   Alphonso shrieked
For joy, and smote his steed and galloped on.

Fronting the gate the standard-bearer holds
His precious charge.   Behind the men divide
In ordered files ; green boyhood presses there,
And waning eld, pleading a youthful soul,
Entreats admission.   All is ardour here,
Hope and brave purposes and minds resolved.
Nor where the weaker sex is left apart
Doth aught of fear find utterance, though perchance
Some paler cheeks might there be seen, some eyes
Big with sad bodings, and some natural tears.
Count Pedro's war-horse in the vacant space
Strikes with impatient hoof the trodden turf,
And gazing round upon the martial show,
Proud of his stately trappings, flings his head,
And snorts and champs the bit, and neighing shrill,
Wakes the near echo with his voice of joy.
The page beside him holds his master's spear
And shield and helmet.   In the castle-gate
Count Pedro stands, his countenance resolved
But mournful, for Favinia on his arm
Hung, passionate with her fears, and held him back.
Go not, she cried, with this deluded crew !
She hath not, Pedro, with her frantic words
Bereft thy faculty,—she is crazed with grief
And her delirium hath infected these :
But, Pedro, thou art calm ; thou dost not share
The madness of the crowd ; thy sober mind
Surveys the danger in its whole extent,
And sees the certain ruin,—for thou know'st

I know thou hast no hope.   Unhappy man,
Why then for this most desperate enterprise
Wilt thou devote thy son, thine only child ?
Not for myself I plead, nor even for thee ;
Thou art a soldier, and thou canst not fear
The face of death ; and I should welcome it
As the best visitant whom Heaven could send.
Not for our lives I speak then,—were they worth
The thought of preservation ;—Nature soon
Must call for them ; the sword that should cut short
Sorrow's slow work were merciful to us.
But spare Alphonso ! there is time and hope
In store for him.   O thou who gavest him life,
Seal not his death, his death and mine at once !

Peace ! he replied : thou know'st there is no choice,
I did not raise the storm ; I cannot turn
Its course aside ! but where yon banner goes
Thy lord must not be absent !   Spare me then,
Favinia, lest I hear thy honoured name
Now first attainted with deserved reproach.
The boy is in God's hands.   He who of yore
Walked with the sons of Judah in the fire,
And from the lions' den drew Daniel forth
Unhurt, can save him,—if it be His will.

Even as he spake, the astonished troop set up
A shout of joy which rung through all the hills.
Alphonso heeds not how they break their ranks
And gather round to greet him ; from his horse
Precipitate and panting off he springs.
Pedro grew pale, and trembled at his sight ;
Favinia clasped her hands, and looking up
To heaven as she embraced the boy, exclaimed,
Lord God, forgive me for my sinful fears ;
Unworthy that I am,—my son, my son !

XII.

THE VOW.

ALWAYS I knew thee for a generous foe,
Pelayo! said the Count ; and in our time
Of enmity, thou too, I know, didst feel
The feud between us was but of the house,
Not of the heart,   Brethren in arms henceforth
We stand or fall together : nor will I
Look to the event with one misgiving thought,—
That were to prove myself unworthy now
Of Heaven's benignant providence, this hour,
Scarcely by less than miracle vouchsafed.
I will believe that we have days in store
Of hope, now risen again as from the dead,—
Of vengeance,—of portentous victory,—
Yea, maugre all unlikelihoods,—of peace.
Let us then here indissolubly knit
Our ancient houses, that those happy days,
When they arrive, may find us more than friends,
And bound by closer than fraternal ties.
Thou hast a daughter, Prince, to whom my heart
Yearns now, as if in winning infancy
Her smiles had been its daily food of love.
I need not tell thee what Alphonso is,—
Thou knowest the boy !
                              Already had that hope,
Replied Pelayo, risen within my soul.
O Thou, who in Thy mercy from the house
Of Moorish bondage hast delivered us,
Fulfil the pious purposes for which
Here, in Thy presence, thus we pledge our hands !

Strange hour to plight espousals ! yielding half
To superstitious thoughts, Favinia cried,
And these strange witnesses !—The times are
        strange,
With thoughtful speech composed her lord replies,
And what thou seest accords with them. This day
Is wonderful ; nor could auspicious Heaven
With fairer or with fitter omen gild

Our enterprise, when strong in heart and hope
We take the field, preparing thus for works
Of piety and love.　Unwillingly
I yielded to my people's general voice,
Thinking that she who with her powerful words
To this excess had roused and kindled them,
Spake from the spirit of her griefs alone,
Not with prophetic impulse.　Be that sin
Forgiven me! and the calm and quiet faith
Which, in the place of incredulity,
Hath filled me, now that seeing I believe,
Doth give of happy end to righteous cause
A presage, not presumptuous, but assured.

　Then Pedro told Pelayo how from vale
To vale the exalted Adosinda went,
Exciting sire and son, in holy war
Conquering or dying, to secure their place
In Paradise : and how reluctantly,
And mourning for his child by his own act
Thus doomed to death, he bade with heavy heart
His banner be brought forth.　Devoid alike
Of purpose and of hope himself, he meant
To march toward the western mountaineers,
Where Odoar by his counsel might direct
Their force conjoined.　Now, said he, we must haste
To Cangas, there, Pelayo, to secure,
With timely speed, I trust in God, thy house.　　·

　Then looking to his men, he cried, Bring forth
The armour which in Wamba's wars I wore.—
Alphonso's heart leapt at the auspicious words.
Count Pedro marked the rising glow of joy,—
Doubly to thee, Alphonso, he pursued,
This day above all other days is blest,
From whence as from a birthday thou wilt date
Thy life in arms !
　　　　　　　Rejoicing in their task,
The servants of the house with emulous love
Dispute the charge.　One brings the cuirass, one
The buckler ; this exultingly displays
The sword, his comrade lifts the helm on high :

The greaves, the gauntlets they divide ; a spur
Seems now to dignify the officious hand
Which for such service bears it to his lord.
Greek artists in the imperial city forged
That splendid armour, perfect in their craft ;
'With curious skill they wrought it, framed alike
To shine amid the pageantry of war,
And for the proof of battle.   Many a time
Alphonso from his nurse's lap had stretched
His infant hands toward it eagerly,
Where gleaming to the central fire it hung
High in the hall ; and many a time had wished
With boyish ardour, that the day were come
When Pedro to his prayers would grant the boon,
His dearest heart's desire.   Count Pedro then
Would smile, and in his heart rejoice to see
The noble instinct manifest itself.
Then too Favinia with maternal pride
Would turn her eyes exulting to her lord,
And in that silent language bid him mark
His spirit in his boy ; all danger then
Was distant, and if secret forethought faint
Of manhood's perils, and the chance of war,
Hateful to mothers, passed across her mind,
The ill remote gave to the present hour
A heightened feeling of secure delight.

No season this for old solemnities,
For wassailry and sport ;—the bath, the bed,
The vigil,—all preparatory rites
Omitted now,—here in the face of Heaven,
Before the vassals of his father's house,
With them in instant peril to partake
The chance of life or death, the heroic boy
Dons his first arms ; the coated scales of steel
Which o'er the tunic to his knees depend,
The hose, the sleeves of mail ; bareheaded then
He stood.   But when Count Pedro took the spurs,
And bent his knee in service to his son,
Alphonso from that gesture half drew back,
Starting in reverence, and a deeper hue
Spread o'er the glow of joy which flushed his cheeks.

Do thou the rest, Pelayo! said the Count;
So shall the ceremony of this hour
Exceed in honour what in form it lacks.
The Prince from Hoya's faithful hand received
The sword; he girt it round the youth, and drew
And placed it in his hand; unsheathing then
His own good falchion, with its burnished blade
He touched Alphonso's neck, and with a kiss
Gave him his rank in arms.
                Thus long the crowd
Had looked intently on, in silence hushed;
Loud and continuous now with one accord,
Shout following shout, their acclamations rose;
Blessings were breathed from every heart, and joy,
Powerful alike in all, which as with force
Of an inebriating cup inspired
The youthful, from the eye of age drew tears.
The uproar died away, when standing forth,
Roderick with lifted hand besought a pause
For speech, and moved towards the youth. I too,
Young baron, he began, must do my part;
Not with prerogative of earthly power,
But as the servant of the living God,
The God of Hosts. This day thou promisest
To die when honour calls thee for thy faith,
For thy liege lord, and for thy native land;
The duties which at birth we all contract,
Are by the high profession of this hour
Made thine especially. Thy noble blood,
The thoughts with which thy childhood had been fed,
And thine own noble nature more than all,
Are sureties for thee. But these dreadful times
Demand a farther pledge; for it hath pleased
The Highest, as He tried His saints of old,
So in the fiery furnace of His wrath
To prove and purify the sons of Spain;
And they must knit their spirits to the proof,
Or sink, for ever lost. Hold forth thy sword,
Young baron, and before thy people take
The vow which, in Toledo's sacred name,
Poor as these weeds bespeak me, I am here
To minister with delegated power.

With reverential awe was Roderick heard
By all, so well authority became
That mien and voice and countenance austere.
Pelayo with complacent eye beheld
The unlooked-for interposal, and the Count
Bends toward Alphonso his approving head.
The youth obedient loosened from his belt
The sword, and looking, while his heart beat fast,
To Roderick, reverently expectant stood.

O noble youth, the royal Goth pursued,
Thy country is in bonds; an impious foe
Oppresses her; he brings with him strange laws,
Strange language, evil customs, and false faith,
And forces them on Spain. Swear that thy soul
Will make no, covenant with these accursed,
But that the sword shall be from this day forth
Thy children's portion, to be handed down
From sire to son, a sacred heritage,
Through every generation, till the work
Be done, and this insulted land hath drunk
In sacrifice, the last invader's blood!

Bear witness, ancient mountains! cried the youth,
And ye, my native streams, who hold your course
For ever;—this dear earth, and yonder sky,
Be witness! for myself I make the vow,
And for my children's children. Here I stand
Their sponsor, binding them in sight of Heaven,
As by a new baptismal sacrament,
To wage hereditary holy war,
Perpetual, patient, persevering war,
Till not one living enemy pollute
The sacred soil of Spain.
                         So as he ceased,
While yet toward the clear blue firmament
His eyes were raised, he lifted to his lips
The sword, with reverent gesture bending then,
Devoutly kissed its cross.
                         And ye! exclaimed
Roderick, as turning to the assembled troop
He motioned with authoritative hand,—
Ye children of the hills and sons of Spain!

Through every heart the rapid feeling ran,—
For us! they answered all with one accord,
And at the word they knelt : people and prince,
The young and old, the father and the son,
At once they knelt ; with one accord they cried,
For us, and for our seed! with one accord
They crossed their fervent arms, and with bent head
Inclined toward that awful voice from whence
The inspiring impulse came. The royal Goth
Made answer, I receive your vow for Spain
And for the Lord of Hosts : your cause is good,
Go forward in His spirit and His strength.

Ne'er in his happiest hours had Roderick
With such commanding majesty dispensed
His princely gifts, as dignified him now,
When with slow movement, solemnly upraised,
Toward the kneeling troop he spread his arms,
As if the expanded soul diffused itself,
And carried to all spirits with the act
Its effluent inspiration. Silently
The people knelt, and when they rose, such awe
Held them in silence, that the eagle's cry,
Who far above them, at her highest flight
A speck scarce visible, gyred round and round,
Was heard distinctly ; and the mountain stream,
Which from the distant glen sent forth its sounds
Wafted upon the wind, grew audible
In that deep hush of feeling, like the voice
Of waters in the stillness of the night.

XIII.

COUNT EUDON.

THAT awful silence still endured, when one,
Who to the northern entrance of the vale
Had turned his casual eye, exclaimed, The Moors!—
For from the forest verge a troop were seen
Hastening toward Pedro's hall. Their forward speed

Was checked when they beheld his banner spread,
And saw his ordered spears in prompt array
Marshalled to meet their coming.   But the pride
Of power and insolence of long command
Pricked on their chief presumptuous : We are come
Late for prevention, cried the haughty Moor,
But never time more fit for punishment !
These unbelieving slaves must feel and know
Their master's arm !—On, faithful Mussulmen,
On—on,—and hew down the rebellious dogs !—
Then as he spurred his steed, Allah is great !
Mahommed is his Prophet ! he exclaimed,
And led the charge.
                        Count Pedro met the chief
In full career : he bore him from his horse
A full spear's-length upon the lance transfixed ;
Then leaving in his breast the mortal shaft,
Passed on, and breaking through the turbaned files,
Opened a path.   Pelayo, who that day
Fought in the ranks afoot, for other war
Yet unequipped, pursued and smote the foe,
But ever on Alphonso at his side
Retained a watchful eye.   The gallant boy
Gave his good sword that hour its earliest taste
Of Moorish blood,—that sword whose hungry edge,
Through the fair course of all his glorious life
From that auspicious day, was fed so well.
Cheap was the victory now for Spain achieved ;
For the first fervour of their zeal inspired
The mountaineers,—the presence of their chiefs,
The sight of all dear objects, all dear ties,
The air they breathed, the soil whereon they trod,
Duty, devotion, faith, and hope and joy.
And little had the misbelievers weened
In such impetuous onset to receive
A greeting deadly as their own intent ;
Victims they thought to find, not men prepared
And eager for the fight ; their confidence
Therefore gave way to wonder, and dismay
Effected what astonishment began.
Scattered before the impetuous mountaineers,
Buckler and spear and scimitar they dropt,

As in precipitate rout they fled before
The Asturian sword : the vales and hills and rocks
Received their blood, and where they fell the wolves
At evening found them.
               From the fight apart
Two Africans had stood, who held in charge
Count Eudon.   When they saw their countrymen
Falter, give way, and fly before the foe,
One turned toward him with malignant rage,
And saying, Infidel ! thou shalt not live
To join their triumph ! aimed against his neck
The moony falchion's point.   His comrade raised
A hasty hand and turned its edge aside,
Yet so that o'er the shoulder glancing down
It scarred him as it passed.   The murderous Moor,
Not tarrying to secure his vengeance, fled ;
While he of milder mood, at Eudon's feet
Fell and embraced his knees.   The mountaineer
Who found them thus, withheld at Eudon's voice
His wrathful hand, and led them to his lord.

Count Pedro and Alphonso and the Prince
Stood on a little rocky eminence
Which overlooked the vale.   Pedro had put
His helmet off, and with sonorous horn
Blew the recall ; for well he knew what thoughts,
Calm as the Prince appeared and undisturbed,
Lay underneath his silent fortitude ;
And how at this eventful juncture speed
Imported more than vengeance.   Thrice he sent
The long-resounding signal forth, which rung
From hill to hill, re-echoing far and wide.
Slow and unwillingly his men obeyed
The swelling horn's reiterated call ;
Repining that a single foe escaped
The retribution of that righteous hour.
With lingering step reluctant from the chase
They turned,—their veins full-swoln, their sinews
      strung
For battle still, their hearts unsatisfied ;
Their swords were dropping still with Moorish
      blood,

And where they wiped their reeking brows, the stain
Of Moorish gore was left.   But when they came
Where Pedro, with Alphonso at his side,
Stood to behold their coming, then they pressed
All emulous, with gratulation round,
Extolling for his deeds that day displayed
The noble boy.   Oh! when had Heaven, they said,
With such especial favour manifest
Illustrated a first essay in arms !
They blessed the father from whose loins he sprung,
The mother at whose happy breast he fed ;
And prayed that their young hero's fields might be
Many, and all like this.
              Thus they indulged
The honest heart, exuberant of love,
When that loquacious joy at once was checked,
For Eudon and the Moor were brought before
Count Pedro.   Both came fearfully and pale,
But with a different fear : the African
Felt at this crisis of his destiny
Such apprehension as without reproach
Might blanch a soldier's cheek, when life and death
Hang on another's will, and helplessly
He must abide the issue.   But the thoughts
Which quailed Count Eudon's heart, and made his
    limbs
Quiver, were of his own unworthiness,
Old enmity, and that he stood in power
Of hated and hereditary foes.
I came not with them willingly ! he cried,
Addressing Pedro and the Prince at once,
Rolling from each to each his restless eyes
Aghast,—the Moor can tell I had no choice ;
They forced me from my castle :—in the fight
They would have slain me :—see, I bleed! The Moor
Can witness that a Moorish scimitar
Inflicted this :—he saved me from worse hurt :—
I did not come in arms :—he knows it all ;—
Speak, man, and let the truth be known to clear
My innocence !
             Thus as he ceased, with fear
And rapid utterance panting open-mouthed,

Count Pedro half repressed a mournful smile,
Wherein compassion seemed to mitigate
His deep contempt.   Methinks, said he, the Moor
Might with more reason look himself to find
An intercessor, than be called upon
To play the pleader's part.   Didst thou then save
The Baron from thy comrades?

                              Let my lord
Show mercy to me, said the Mussulman,
As I am free from falsehood.   We were left,
I and another, holding him in charge ;
My fellow would have slain him when he saw
How the fight fared : I turned the scimitar
Aside, and trust that life will be the meed
For life by me preserved.

                         Nor shall thy trust,
Rejoined the Count, be vain.   Say farther now,
From whence ye came?—your orders what?—what
      force
In Gegio? and if others like yourselves
Are in the field?

                   The African replied,
We came from Gegio, ordered to secure
This Baron on the way, and seek thee here
To bear thee hence in bonds.   A messenger
From Cordoba, whose speed denoted well
He came with urgent tidings, was the cause
Of this our sudden movement.   We went forth
Three hundred men ; an equal force was sent
For Cangas, on like errand as I ween.
Four hundred in the city then were left.
If other force be moving from the south,
I know not, save that all appearances
Denote alarm and vigilance.

                              The Prince
Fixed upon Eudon then his eye severe ;
Baron, he said, the die of war is cast ;
What part art thou prepared to take? against,
Or with the oppressor?

                        Not against my friends,—
Not against you !—the irresolute wretch replied, .
Hasty, yet faltering in his fearful speech :

But—have ye weighed it well?—It is not yet
Too late,—their numbers,—their victorious force,
Which hath already trodden in the dust
The sceptre of the Goths:—the throne destroyed,—
Our towns subdued,—our country overrun,—
The people to the yoke of their new lords
Resigned in peace.—Can I not mediate?—
Were it not better through my agency
To gain such terms,—such honourable terms,—

Terms! cried Pelayo, cutting short at once
That dastard speech, and checking, ere it grew
Too powerful for restraint, the incipient wrath
Which in indignant murmurs breathing round,
Rose like a gathering storm, learn thou what terms
Asturias, this day speaking by my voice,
Doth constitute to be the law between
Thee and thy country.   Our portentous age,
As with an earthquake's desolating force,
Hath loosened and disjointed the whole frame
Of social order, and she calls not now
For service with the force of sovereign.will.
That which was common duty in old times,
Becomes an arduous, glorious virtue now;
And every one, as between hell and heaven,
In free election must be left to choose.
Asturias asks not of thee to partake
The cup which we have pledged; she claims from
          none
The dauntless fortitude, the mind resolved,
Which only God can give;—therefore such peace
As thou canst find where all around is war,
She leaves thee to enjoy.   But think not, Count,
That because thou art weak, one valiant arm,
One generous spirit must be lost to Spain!
The vassal owes no service to the lord
Who to his country doth acknowledge none.
The summons which thou hast not heart to give,
I and Count Pedro over thy domains
Will send abroad; the vassals who were thine
Will fight beneath our banners, and our wants
Shall from thy lands, as from a patrimony

Which hath reverted to the common stock,
Be fed : such tribute, too, as to the Moors
'Thou renderest, we will take : It is the price
Which in this land for weakness must be paid
While evil stars prevail.   And mark me, chief !
Fear is a treacherous counsellor ! I know
Thou thinkest that beneath his horses' hoofs
The Moor will trample our poor numbers down ;
But join not, in contempt of us and Heaven,
His multitudes ! for if thou shouldst be found
Against thy country, on the readiest tree
Those recreant bones shall rattle in the wind
When the birds have left them bare.
                                        As thus he spake,
Count Eudon heard and trembled : every joint
Was loosened, every fibre of his flesh
Thrilled, and from every pore effused, cold sweat
Clung on his quivering limbs. Shame forced it forth,
Envy, and inward consciousness, and fear
Predominant, which stifled in his heart
Hatred and rage.   Before his livid lips
Could shape to utterance their essayed reply,
Compassionately Pedro interposed.
Go, Baron, to the castle, said the Count ;
There let thy wound be looked to, and consult
Thy better mind at leisure.   Let this Moor
Attend upon thee there, and when thou wilt,
Follow thy fortunes.—To Pelayo then
He turned, and saying, All too long, O Prince,
Hath this unlooked-for conflict held thee here,—
He bade his gallant men begin their march.

Flushed with success, and in auspicious hour,
'The mountaineers set forth.   Blessings and prayers
Pursued them at their parting, and the tears
Which fell were tears of fervour, not of grief.
Tho sun was verging to the western slope
Of heaven, but they till midnight travelled on ;
Renewing then at early dawn their way,
They held their unremitting course from morn
Till latest eve, such urgent cause impelled ;
And night had closed around, when to the vale

Where Sella in her ampler bed receives
Pionia's stream they came.   Massive and black
Pelayo's castle there was seen ; its lines
And battlements against the deep blue sky
Distinct in solid darkness visible.
No light is in the tower.   Eager to know
The worst, and with that fatal certainty
To terminate intolerable dread,
He spurred his courser forward.   All his fears
Too surely are fulfilled,—for open stand
The doors, and mournfully at times a dog
Fills with his howling the deserted hall.
A moment overcome with wretchedness,
Silent Pelayo stood ! recovering then,
Lord God, resigned he cried, Thy will be done !

XIV.

THE RESCUE.

COUNT, said Pelayo, Nature hath assigned
Two sovereign remedies for human grief ;
Religion, surest, firmest, first and best,
Strength to the weak and to the wounded balm ;
And strenuous action next.   Think not I came
With unprovided heart.   My noble wife,
In the last solemn words, the last farewell
With which she charged her secret messenger,
Told me that whatsoe'er was my resolve,
She bore a mind prepared.   And well I know
The evil, be it what it may, hath found
In her a courage equal to the hour.
Captivity, or death, or what worse pangs,
She in her children may be doomed to feel,
Will never make that steady soul repent
Its virtuous purpose.   I too did not cast
My single life into the lot, but knew
These dearer pledges on the die were set ;
And if the worst have fallen, I shall but bear
That in my breast, which, with transfiguring power
E

Of piety, makes chastening sorrow take
The form of hope, and sees, in Death, the friend
And the restoring Angel.   We must rest
Perforce, and wait what tidings night may bring,
Haply of comfort.   Ho there ! kindle fires,
And see if aught of hospitality
Can yet within these mournful walls be found !

   Thus while he spake, lights were descried far off
Moving among the trees, and coming sounds
Were heard as of a distant multitude.
Anon a company of horse and foot,
Advancing in disorderly array,
Came up the vale ; before them and beside
Their torches flashed on Sella's rippling stream ;
Now gleamed through chestnut groves, emerging
    now,
O'er their huge boughs and radiated leaves
Cast broad and bright a transitory glare.
That sight inspired with strength the mountaineers ;
All sense of weariness, all wish for rest
At once were gone ; impatient in desire
Of second victory alert they stood ;
And when the hostile symbols, which from far
Imagination to their wish had shaped,
Vanished in nearer vision, high-wrought hope
Departing, left the spirit palled and blank.
No turbaned race, no sons of Africa
Were they who now came winding up the vale
As waving wide before their horses' feet
The torch-light floated, with its hovering glare
Blackening the incumbent and surrounding night.
Helmet and breastplate glittered as they came
And spears erect ; and nearer as they drew
Were the loose folds of female garments seen
On those who led the company.   Who then
Had stood beside Pelayo, might have heard
The beating of his heart.
               But vainly there
Sought he with wistful eye the well-known forms
Beloved ; and plainly might it now be seen
That from some bloody conflict they returned

Victorious,—for at every saddle-bow
A gory head was hung. Anon they stopped,
Levelling in quick alarm their ready spears.
Hold ! who goes there? cried one. A hundred
    tongues
Sent forth with one accord the glad reply,
Friends and Asturians. Onward moved the lights,—
The people knew their lord.

                    Then what a shout
Rung through the valley ! From their clay-built
    nests,
Beneath the overbrowing battlements,
Now first disturbed, the affrighted martins flew,
And uttering notes of terror short and shrill,
Amid the yellow glare and lurid smoke
Wheeled giddily. Then plainly was it shown
How well the vassals loved their generous lord,
How like a father the Asturian Prince
Was dear. They crowded round ; they clasped
    his knees ;
They snatched his hand; they fell upon his neck,—
They wept ;—they blest Almighty Providence,
Which had restored him thus from bondage free ;
God was with them and their good cause, they said ;
His hand was here,—His shield was over them,—
His spirit was abroad,—His power displayed :
And pointing to their bloody trophies then,
They told Pelayo there he might behold
The first-fruits of the harvest they should soon
Reap in the field of war ! Benignantly,
With voice and look and gesture, did the Prince
To these warm greetings of tumultuous joy
Respond ; and sure if at that moment aught
Could for a while have overpowered those fears
Which from the inmost heart o'er all his frame
Diffused their chilling influence, worthy pride,
And sympathy of love and joy and hope,
Had then possessed him wholly. Even now
His spirit rose ; the sense of power, the sight
Of his brave people, ready where he led
To fight their country's battles, and the thought
Of instant action, and deliverance,—

If Heaven, which thus far had protected him,
Should favour still,—revived his heart, and gave
Fresh impulse to its spring. In vain he sought
Amid that turbulent greeting to inquire
Where Gaudiosa was, his children where,
Who called them to the field, who captained them;
And how these women, thus with arms and death
Environed, came amid their company?
For yet, amid the fluctuating light
And tumult of the crowd, he knew them not.

Guisla was one. The Moors had found in her
A willing and concerted prisoner.
Gladly to Gegio, to the renegade
On whom her loose and shameless love was bent,
Had she set forth; and in her heart she cursed
The busy spirit, who, with powerful call
Rousing Pelayo's people, led them on
In quick pursual, and victoriously
Achieved the rescue, to her mind perverse
Unwelcome as unlooked for. With dismay
She recognised her brother, dreaded now
More than he once was dear; her countenance
Was turned toward him—not with eager joy
To court his sight, and meeting its first glance,
Exchange delightful welcome, soul with soul;
Hers was the conscious eye, that cannot choose
But look to what it fears. She could not shun
His presence, and the rigid smile constrained,
With which she coldly dressed her features, ill
Concealed her inward thoughts, and the despite
Of obstinate guilt and unrepentant shame.
Sullenly thus upon her mule she sate,
Waiting the greeting which she did not dare
Bring on. But who is she that at her side,
Upon a stately war-horse eminent,
Holds the loose rein with careless hand? A helm
Presses the clusters of her flaxen hair;
The shield is on her arm; her breast is mailed;
A sword-belt is her girdle, and right well
It may be seen that sword hath done its work
To-day, for upward from the wrist her sleeve

Is stiff with blood.   An unregardant eye,
As one whose thoughts were not of earth, she cast
Upon the turmoil round.   One countenance
So strongly marked, so passion-worn was there,
That it recalled her mind.   Ha ! Maccabee !
Lifting her arm, exultingly she cried,
Did I not tell thee we should meet in joy?
Well, brother, hast thou done thy part,—I too
Have not been wanting !   Now be His the praise,
From whom the impulse came !
                              That startling call,
That voice so well remembered, touched the Goth
With timely impulse now ; for he had seen
His mother's face,—and at her sight, the past
And present mingled like a frightful dream,
Which from some dread reality derives
Its deepest horror.   Adosinda's voice
Dispersed the waking vision.   Little deemed
Rusilla at that moment that the child,
For whom her supplications day and night
Were offered, breathed the living air.   Her heart
Was calm ; her placid countenance, though grief
Deeper than time had left its traces there,
Retained its dignity serene ; yet when
Siverian, pressing through the people, kissed
Her reverend hand, some quiet tears ran down.
As she approached the Prince, the crowd made way
Respectful.   The maternal smile which bore
Her greeting, from Pelayo's heart at once
Dispelled its boding.   What he would have asked
She knew, and bending from her palfrey down,
Told him that they for whom he looked were safe,
And that in secret he should hear the rest.

XV.

RODERICK AT CANGAS.

How calmly gliding through the dark-blue sky
The midnight moon ascends ! Her placid beams
Through thinly scattered leaves and boughs gro-
    tesque,
Mottle with mazy shades the orchard slope ;
Here, o'er the chestnut's fretted foliage grey
And massy, motionless they spread ; here shine
Upon the crags, deepening with blacker night
Their chasms ; and there the glittering argentry
Ripples and glances on the confluent streams.
A lovelier, purer light than that of day
Rests on the hills ; and oh, how awfully
Into that deep and tranquil firmament
The summits of Auseva rise serene !
The watchman on the battlements partakes
The stillness of the solemn hour ; he feels
The silence of the earth, the endless sound
Of flowing water soothes him, and the stars,
Which in that brightest moonlight well-nigh
    quenched
Scarce visible, as in the utmost depth
Of yonder sapphire infinite, are seen,
Draw on with elevating influence
Toward eternity the attempered mind.
Musing on worlds beyond the grave he stands,
And to the Virgin Mother silently
Prefers her hymn of praise.
               The mountaineers
Before the castle, round their mouldering fires,
Lie on the hearth outstretched. Pelayo's hall
Is full, and he upon his careful couch
Hears all around the deep and long-drawn breath
Of sleep : for gentle night hath brought to these
Perfect and undisturbed repose, alike
Of corporal powers and inward faculty.
Wakeful the while he lay, yet more by hope
Than grief or anxious thoughts possessed,—though
    grief

For Guisla's guilt, which freshened in his heart
The memory of their wretched mother's crime,
Still made its presence felt, like the dull sense
Of some perpetual inward malady;
And the whole peril of the future lay
Before him clearly seen.   He had heard all;
How that unworthy sister, obstinate
In wrong and shameless, rather seemed to woo
The upstart renegado than to wait
His wooing; how, as guilt to guilt led on,
Spurning at gentle admonition first,
When Gaudiosa hopelessly forbore
From further counsel, then in sullen mood
Resentful, Guisla soon began to hate
The virtuous presence before which she felt
Her nature how inferior, and her fault
How foul.   Despiteful thus she grew, because
Humbled yet unrepentant.   Who could say
To what excess bad passions might impel
A woman thus possessed?   She could not fail
To mark Siverian's absence, for what end
Her conscience but too surely had divined;
And Gaudiosa, well aware that all
To the vile paramour was thus made known,
Had to safe hiding-place with timely fear
Removed her children.   Well the event had
     proved
How needful was that caution; for at night
She sought the mountain solitudes, and morn
Beheld Numacian's soldiers at the gate.
Yet did not sorrow in Pelayo's heart
For this domestic shame prevail that hour,
Nor gathering danger weigh his spirit down.
The anticipated meeting put to flight
These painful thoughts; to-morrow will restore
All whom his heart holds dear; his wife beloved,
No longer now remembered for regret,
Is present to his soul with hope and joy;
His inward eye beholds Favila's form
In opening youth robust, and Hermesind,
His daughter, lovely as a budding rose;
Their images beguile the hours of night,

Till with the earliest morning he may seek
Their secret hold.

           The nightingale not yet
Had ceased her song, nor had the early lark
Her dewy nest forsaken, when the Prince
Upward beside Pionia took his way
Toward Auseva.   Heavily to him,
Impatient for the morrow's happiness,
Long night had lingered, but it seemed more long
To Roderick's aching heart.   He too had watched
For dawn, and seen the earliest break of day,
And heard its earliest sounds ; and when the Prince
Went forth, the melancholy man was seen
With pensive pace upon Pionia's side
Wandering alone and slow.   For he had left
The wearying place of his unrest, that morn
With its cold dews might bathe his throbbing brow,
And with its breath allay the feverish heat
That burnt within.   Alas ! the gales of morn
Reach not the fever of a wounded heart !
How shall he meet his mother's eye, how make
His secret known, and from that voice revered
Obtain forgiveness,—all that he has now
To ask, ere on the lap of earth in peace
He lay his head resigned?   In silent prayer
He supplicated Heaven to strengthen him
Against that trying hour, there seeking aid
Where all who seek shall find ; and thus his soul
Received support, and gathered fortitude,
Never than now more needful, for the hour
Was nigh.   He saw Siverian drawing near,
And with a dim but quick foreboding met
The good old man ; yet when he heard him say
My lady sends to seek thee, like a knell
To one expecting and prepared for death,
But fearing the dread point that hastens on,
It smote his heart.   He followed silently,
And knit his suffering spirit to the proof.

    He went resolved to tell his mother all,
Fall at her feet, and drinking the last dregs
Of bitterness, receive the only good

Earth had in store for him.   Resolved for this
He went ; yet was it a relief to find
That painful resolution must await
A fitter season, when no eye but Heaven's
Might witness to their mutual agony.
Count Julian's daughter with Rusilla sate ;
Both had been weeping, both were pale, but calm.
With head as for humility abased
Roderick approached, and bending, on his breast
He crossed his humble arms.   Rusilla rose
In reverence to the priestly character,
And with a mournful eye regarding him,
Thus she began : Good father, I have heard
From my old faithful servant and true friend,
Thou didst reprove the inconsiderate tongue,
That in the anguish of its spirit poured
A curse upon my poor unhappy child.
O Father Maccabee, this is a hard world,
And hasty in its judgments !   Time has been,
When not a tongue within the Pyrenees
Dared whisper in dispraise of Roderick's name
Lest, if the conscious air had caught the sound,
The vengeance of the honest multitude
Should fall upon the traitorous head, or brand
For life-long infamy the lying lips.
Now if a voice be raised in his behalf,
'Tis noted for a wonder, and the man
Who utters the strange speech shall be admired
For such excess of Christian charity.
Thy Christian charity hath not been lost ;—
Father, I feel its virtue :—it hath been
Balm to my heart ;—with words and grateful tears,—
All that is left me now for gratitude,—
I thank thee, and beseech thee in thy prayers
That thou wilt still remember Roderick's name.

Roderick so long had to this hour looked on,
That when the actual point of trial came,
Torpid and numbed it found him ; cold he grew,
And as the vital spirits to the heart
Retreated, o'er his withered countenance,
Deathy and damp, a whiter paleness spread.

Unmoved the while, the inward feeling seemed,
Even in such dull insensibility
As gradual age brings on, or slow disease,
Beneath whose progress lingering life survives
The power of suffering. Wondering at himself,
Yet gathering confidence, he raised his eyes,
Then slowly shaking as he bent his head,
O venerable lady, he replied,
If aught may comfort that unhappy soul,
It must be thy compassion, and thy prayers.
She whom he most hath wronged, she who alone
On earth can grant forgiveness for his crime,
She hath forgiven him ; and thy blessing now
Were all that he could ask,—all that could bring
Profit or consolation to his soul,
If he hath been, as sure we may believe,
A penitent sincere.
                         Oh, had he lived,
Replied Rusilla, never penitence
Had equalled his ! full well I know his heart,
Vehement in all things. He would on himself
Have wreaked such penance as had reached the
      height
Of fleshly suffering ;—yea, which being told
With its portentous rigour should have made
The memory of his fault, o'erpowered and lost
In shuddering pity and astonishment,
Fade like a feebler horror. Otherwise
Seemed good to Heaven. I murmur not, nor doubt
The boundless mercy of redeeming love.
For sure I trust that not in his offence
Hardened and reprobate was my lost son,
A child of wrath, cut off !—that dreadful thought,
Not even amid the first fresh wretchedness,
When the ruin first burst around me like a flood,
Assailed my soul. I ever deemed his fall
An act of sudden madness ; and this day
Hath in unlooked-for confirmation given
A livelier hope, a more assuréd faith.
Smiling benignant then amid her tears,
She took Florinda by the hand, and said,
I little thought that I should live to bless

Count Julian's daughter ! She hath brought to me
The last, the best, the only comfort earth
Could minister to this afflicted heart,
And my grey hairs may now unto the grave
Go down in peace.

                Happy, Florinda cried,
Are they for whom the grave hath peace in store !
The wrongs they have sustained, the woes they bear,
Pass not that holy threshold, where Death heals
The broken heart. O lady, thou may'st trust
In humble hope, through Him who on the Cross
Gave His atoning blood for lost mankind,
To meet beyond the grave thy child forgiven.
I too with Roderick there may interchange
Forgiveness. But the grief which wastes away
This mortal frame, hastening the happy hour
Of my enlargement, is but a light part
Of what my soul endures !—that grief hath lost
Its sting :—I have a keener sorrow here,—
One which,—but God forfend that dire event,—
May pass with me the portals of the grave,
And with a thought, like sin which cannot die,
Embitter heaven. My father hath renounced
His hope in Christ ! It was his love for me
Which drove him to perdition.—I was born
To ruin all who loved me,—all I loved !
Perhaps I sinned in leaving him ;—that fear
Rises within me to disturb the peace
Which I should else have found.

                    To Roderick then
The pious mourner turned her suppliant eyes :
O father, there is virtue in thy prayers !—
I do beseech thee offer them to Heaven
In his behalf ! For Roderick's sake, for mine,
Wrestle with Him whose name is Merciful,
That Julian may with penitence be touched,
And clinging to the Cross, implore that grace ·
Which ne'er was sought in vain. For Roderick's
    sake
And mine, pray for him ! We have been the cause
Of his offence ! What other miseries
May from that same unhappy source have risen,

Are earthly, temporal, reparable all ;—
But if a soul be lost through our misdeeds,
That were eternal evil !   Pray for him,
Good Father Maccabee, and be thy prayers
More fervent, as the deeper is the crime.

While thus Florinda spake, the dog who lay
Before Rusilla's feet, eyeing him long
And wistfully, had recognised at length,
Changed as he was and in those sordid weeds,
His royal master.   And he rose and licked
His withered hand, and earnestly looked up
With eyes whose human meaning did not need
The aid of speech ; and moaned, as if at once
To court and chide the long-withheld caress.
A feeling uncommixed with sense of guilt
Or shame, yet painfullest, thrilled through the King;
But he to self-control now long inured,
Repressed his rising heart, nor other tears,
Full as his struggling bosom was, let fall
Than seemed to follow on Florinda's words.
Looking toward her then, yet so that still
He shunned the meeting of her eye, he said,
Virtuous and pious as thou art, and ripe
For heaven, O lady, I must think the man
Hath not by his good angel been cast off
For whom thy supplications rise.   The Lord,
Whose justice doth in its unerring course
Visit the children for the sire's offence,
Shall He not in His boundless mercy hear
The daughter's prayer, and for her sake restore
The guilty parent !   My soul shall with thine
In earnest and continual duty join.—
How deeply, how devoutly, He will know
To whom the cry is raised !
                              Thus having said,
Deliberately, in self-possession still,
Himself from that most painful interview
Dispeeding, he withdrew.   The watchful dog
Followed his footsteps close.   But he retired
Into the thickest grove ; there yielding way
To his o'erburthened nature, from all eyes

Apart, he cast himself upon the ground,
And threw his arms around the dog, and cried,
While tears streamed down, Thou, Theron, then
    hast known
Thy poor lost master,—Theron, none but thou!

XVI.

COVADONGA.

MEANTIME Pelayo up the vale pursued
Eastward his way, before the sun had climbed
Auseva's brow, or shed his silvering beams
Upon Europa's summit, where the snows
Through all revolving seasons hold their seat.
A happy man he went, his heart at rest,
Of hope and virtue and affection full,
To all exhilarating influences
Of earth and heaven alive. With kindred joy
He heard the lark, who from her airy height,
On twinkling pinions poised, poured forth profuse,
In thrilling sequence of exuberant song,
As one whose joyous nature overflowed
With life and power, her rich and rapturous strain.
The early bee, buzzing along the way,
From flower to flower, bore gladness on its wing
To his rejoicing sense ; and he pursued,
With quickened eye alert, the frolic hare,
Where from the green herb in her wanton path
She brushed away the dews. For he long time,
Far from his home and from his native hills,
Had dwelt in bondage ; and the mountain breeze,
Which he had with the breath of infancy
Inhaled, such impulse to his heart restored,
As if the seasons had rolled back, and life
Enjoyed a second spring.
               Through fertile fields
He went, by cots with pear-trees overbowered,
Or spreading to the sun their trellised vines ;
Through orchards now, and now by thymy banks,
Where wooden hives in some warm nook were hid

From wind and shower ; and now through shadowy
    paths,
Where hazels fringed Pionia's vocal stream ;
Till where the loftier hills to narrower bound
Confine the vale, he reached those huts remote
Which should hereafter to the noble line
Of Soto origin and name impart :
A gallant lineage, long in fields of war
And faithful chronicler's enduring page
Blazoned : but most by him illustrated,
Avid of gold, yet greedier of renown,
Whom not the spoils of Atabalipa
Could satisfy insatiate, nor the fame
Of that wide empire overthrown appease ;
But he to Florida's disastrous shores
In evil hour his gallant comrades led,
Through savage woods and swamps, and hostile
    tribes,
The Apalachian arrows, and the snares
Of wilier foes, hunger, and thirst, and toil ;
Till from ambition's feverish dream the touch
Of Death awoke him ; and when he had seen
The fruit of all his treasures, all his toil,
Foresight, and long endurance, fade away,
Earth to the restless one refusing rest,
In the great river's midland bed he left
His honoured bones.
              A mountain rivulet,
Now calm and lovely in its summer course,
Held by those huts its everlasting way
Towards Pionia.   They whose flocks and herds
Drink of its water call it Deva.   Here
Pelayo southward up the ruder vale
Traced it, his guide unerring.   Amid heaps
Of mountain wreck, on either side thrown high
The wide-spread traces of its wintry night,
The tortuous channel wound ; o'er beds of sand
Here silently it flows ; here from the rock
Rebutted, curls and eddies ; plunges here
Precipitate ; here roaring among crags,
It leaps and foams and whirls and hurries on.
Grey alders here and bushy hazels hid

The mossy side ; their wreathed and knotted feet
Bared by the current, now against its force
Repaying the support they found, upheld
The bank secure.   Here, bending to the stream,
The birch fantastic stretched its rugged trunk,
Tall and erect from whence, as from their base,
Each like a tree, its silver branches grew.
The cherry here hung for the birds of heaven
Its rosy fruit on high.   The elder there
Its purple berries o'er the water bent,
Heavily hanging.   Here, amid the brook,
Grey as the stone to which it clung, half root,
Half trunk, the young ash rises from the rock ;
And there its parent lifts a lofty head,
And spreads its graceful boughs ;   the passing
  wind
With twinkling motion lifts the silent leaves,
And shakes its rattling tufts.
      Soon had the Prince
Behind him left the farthest dwelling-place
Of man ; no fields of waving corn were here,
Nor wicker storehouse for the autumnal grain,
Vineyard, nor bowery fig, nor fruitful grove ;
Only the rocky vale, the mountain stream,
Incumbent crags, and hills that over hills
Arose on either hand, here hung with woods,
Here rich with heath, that o'er some smooth
  ascent
Its purple glory spread, or golden gorse ;
Bare here, and striated with many a hue,
Scored by the wintry rain ; by torrents here
Riven, and with overhanging rocks abrupt.
Pelayo, upward as he cast his eyes
Where crags loose-hanging o'er the narrow pass
Impended, there beheld his country's strength
Insuperable, and in his heart rejoiced.
Oh, that the Mussulman were here, he cried,
With all his myriads !   While thy day endures,
Moor ! thou may'st lord it in the plains ; but here
Hath Nature for the free and brave prepared
A sanctuary, where no oppressor's power,
No might of human tyranny can pierce.

The tears which started then sprang not alone
From lofty thoughts of elevating joy;
For love and admiration had their part,
And virtuous pride.   Here then thou hast retired,
My Gaudiosa! in his heart he said;
Excellent woman! ne'er was richer boon
By fate benign to favoured man indulged,
Than when thou wert before the face of Heaven
Given me to be my children's mother, brave
And virtuous as thou art!   Here thou hast fled,
Thou who wert nurst in palaces, to dwell
In rocks and mountain caves!—The thought was
      proud,
Yet not without a sense of inmost pain;
For never had Pelayo till that hour
So deeply felt the force of solitude.
High overhead the eagle soared serene,
And the grey lizard on the rocks below
Basked in the sun : no living creature else
In this remotest wilderness was seen;
Nor living voice was there,—only the flow
Of Deva, and the rushing of its springs
Long in the distance heard, which nearer now,
With endless repercussion deep and loud,
Throbbed on the dizzy sense.
                        The ascending vale,
Long straitened by the narrowing mountains, here
Was closed.   In front a rock, abrupt and bare,
Stood eminent, in height exceeding far
All edifice of human power, by king
Or caliph, or barbaric sultan reared,
Or mightier tyrants of the world of old,
Assyrian or Egyptian, in their pride;
Yet far above, beyond the reach of sight,
Swell after swell, the heathery mountain rose.
Here, in two sources, from the living rock
The everlasting springs of Deva gushed.
Upon a smooth and grassy plat below,
By Nature there as for an altar drest,
They joined their sister stream, which from the earth
Welled silently.   In such a scene rude man
With pardonable error might have knelt,

Feeling a present Deity, and made
His offering to the fountain Nymph devout.

   The arching rock disclosed above the springs
A cave, where hugest son of giant birth,
That e'er of old in forest of romance
'Gainst knights and ladies waged discourteous war,
Erect within the portal might have stood.
The broken stone allowed for hand and foot
No difficult ascent, above the base
In height a tall man's stature, measured thrice.
No holier spot than Covadonga Spain
Boasts in her wide extent, though all her realms
Be with the noblest blood of martyrdom
In elder or in later days enriched,
And glorified with tales of heavenly aid
By many a miracle made manifest ;
Nor in the heroic annals of her fame
Doth she show forth a scene of more renown.
Then, save the hunter, drawn in keen pursuit
Beyond his wonted haunts, or shepherd's boy,
Following the pleasure of his straggling flock,
None knew the place.
                              Pelayo, when he saw
Those glittering sources and their sacred cave,
Took from his side the bugle silver-tipt,
And with a breath long drawn and slow expired
Sent forth that strain, which, echoing from the walls
Of Cangas, wont to tell his glad return
When from the chase he came.   At the first sound
Favila started in the cave, and cried,
My father s horn !—A sudden flush suffused
Hermesind's cheek, and she with quickened eye
Looked eager to her mother silently ;
But Gaudiosa trembled and grew pale,
Doubting her sense deceived.   A second time
The bugle breathed its well-known notes abroad ;
And Hermesind around her mother's neck
Threw her white arms, and earnestly exclaimed,
'Tis he !—But when a third and broader blast
Rung in the echoing archway, ne'er did wand,
With magic power endued, call up a sight

So strange, as sure in that wild solitude
It seemed, when from the bowels of the rock
The mother and her children hastened forth ;
She in the sober charms and dignity
Of womanhood mature, nor verging yet
Upon decay ; in gesture like a queen,
Such inborn and habitual majesty
Ennobled all her steps,—or priestess, chosen
Because within such faultless work of heaven
Inspiring Deity might seem to make
Its habitation known ;—Favila such
In form and stature as the Sea Nymph's son,
When that wise Centaur from his cave well-pleased
Beheld the boy divine his growing strength
Against some shaggy lionet essay,
And fixing in the half-grown mane his hands,
Roll with him in fierce dalliance intertwined.
But like a creature of some higher sphere
His sister came ; she scarcely touched the rock,
So light was Hermesind's aërial speed.
Beauty and grace and innocence in her
In heavenly union shone.   One who had held
The faith of elder Greece, would sure have thought
She was some glorious nymph of seed divine,
Oread or dryad, of Diana's train
The youngest and the loveliest : yea, she seemed
Angel, or soul beatified, from realms
Of bliss, on errand of parental love
To earth re-sent,—if tears and trembling limbs
With such celestial natures might consist.

Embraced by all, in turn embracing each,
The husband and the father for a while
Forgot his country and all things beside :
Life hath few moments of such pure delight,
Such foretaste of the perfect joy of heaven.
And when the thought recurred of sufferings past,
Perils which threatened still, and arduous toil
Yet to be undergone, remembered griefs
Heightened the present happiness ; and hope
Upon the shadows of futurity
Shone like the sun upon the morning mists,

When driven before his rising rays they roll,
And melt and leave the prospect bright and clear.

When now Pelayo's eyes had drunk their fill
Of love from those dear faces, he went up
To view the hiding-place.   Spacious it was
As that Sicilian cavern in the hill
Wherein earth-shaking Neptune's giant son
Duly at eve was wont to fold his flock,
Ere the wise Ithacan, over that brute force
By wiles prevailing, for a lifelong night
Sealed his broad eye.   The healthful air had here
Free entrance, and the cheerful light of heaven ;
But at the end, an opening in the floor
Of rock disclosed a wider vault below,
Which never sunbeam visited, nor breath
Of vivifying morning came to cheer.
No light was there but that which from above
In dim reflection fell, or found its way,
Broken and quivering, through the glassy stream,
Where through the rock it gushed.   That shadowy
      light
Sufficed to show, where from their secret bed
The waters issued ; with whose rapid course,
And with whose everlasting cataracts
Such motion to the chill damp atmosphere
Was given, as if the solid walls of rock
Were shaken with the sound.
                              Glad to respire
The upper air, Pelayo hastened back
From that drear den. Look ! Hermesind exclaimed,
Taking her father's hand, thou hast not seen
My chamber :—See !—did ever ring-dove choose
In so secure a nook her hiding-place,   .
Or build a warmer nest? 'Tis fragrant too,
As warm, and not more sweet than soft; for thyme
And myrtle with the elastic heath are laid,
And, over all, this dry and pillowy moss.—
Smiling she spake.   Pelayo kissed the child,
And, sighing, said within himself, I trust
In Heaven, whene'er thy May of life is come,
Sweet bird, that thou shalt have a blither bower !

Fitlier, he thought, such chamber might beseem
Some hermit of Hilarion's school austere,
Or old Antonius, he who from the hell
Of his bewildered phantasy saw fiends
In actual vision, a foul throng grotesque
Of all horrific shapes and forms obscene
Crowd in broad day before his open eyes.
That feeling cast a momentary shade
Of sadness o'er his soul.   But deeper thoughts,
If he might have foreseen the things to come,
Would there have filled him ; for within that cave
His own remains were one day doomed to find
Their final place of rest ; and in that spot,
Where that dear child with innocent delight
Had spread her mossy couch, the sepulchre
Shall in the consecrated rock be hewn,
Where with Alphonso, her beloved lord,
Laid side by side, must Hermesind partake
The everlasting marriage-bed, when he,
Leaving a name perdurable on earth,
Hath changed his earthly for a heavenly crown.
Dear child, upon that fated spot she stood,
In all the beauty of her opening youth,
In health's rich bloom, in virgin innocence,
While her eyes sparkled and her heart o'erflowed
With pure and perfect joy of filial love.

Many a slow century since that day hath filed
Its course, and countless multitudes have trod
With pilgrim feet that consecrated cave ;
Yet not in all those ages, amid all
The untold concourse, hath one breast been swollen
With such emotions as Pelayo felt
That hour.   O Gaudiosa, he exclaimed,
And thou couldst seek for shelter here, amid
This awful solitude, in mountain caves !
Thou noble spirit !   Oh, when hearts like thine
Grow on this sacred soil, would it not be
In me, thy husband, double infamy,
And tenfold guilt, if I despaired of Spain?
In all her visitations, favouring Heaven
Hath left her still the unconquerable mind ;

And thus being worthy of redemption, sure
Is she to be redeemed.
                              Beholding her
Through tears he spake, and pressed upon her lips
A kiss of deepest love.   Think ever thus,
She answered, and that faith will give the power
In which it trusts.   When to this mountain hold
These children, thy dear images, I brought,
I said within myself, where should they fly
But to the bosom of their native hills?
I brought them here as to a sanctuary,
Where, for the temple's sake, the indwelling God
Would guard His supplicants.   Oh, my dear lord
Proud as I was to know that they were thine,
Was it a sin if I almost believed
That Spain, her destiny being linked with theirs,
Must save the precious charge?
                                      So let us think,
The chief replied, so feel and teach and act.
Spain is our common parent: let the sons
Be to the parent true, and in her strength
And Heaven, their sure deliverance they will find.

XVII.

RODERICK AND SIVERIAN.

O HOLIEST Mary, maid and mother! thou
In Covadonga, at thy rocky shrine,
Hast witnessed whatsoe'er of human bliss
Heart can conceive most perfect!   Faithful love,
Long crossed by envious stars, hath there attained
Its crown, in endless matrimony given;
The youthful mother there hath to the font
Her first-born borne, and there, with deeper sense
Of gratitude for that dear babe redeemed
From threatening death, returned to pay her vows.
But ne'er on nuptial, nor baptismal day,
Nor from their grateful pilgrimage discharged,
Did happier group their way down Deva's vale

Rejoicing hold, than this blest family,
O'er whom the mighty Spirit of the Land
Spread his protecting wings. The children, free
In youthhead's happy season from all cares
That might disturb the hour, yet capable
Of that intense and unalloyed delight
Which childhood feels when it enjoys again
The dear parental presence long deprived;
Nor were the parents now less blessed than they,
Even to the height of human happiness;
For Gaudiosa and her lord that hour
Let no misgiving thoughts intrude: she fixed
Her hopes on him, and his were fixed on heaven;
And hope in that courageous heart derived
Such rooted strength and confidence assured
In righteousness, that 'twas to him like faith—
An everlasting sunshine of the soul,
Illumining and quickening all its powers.

But on Pionia's side meantime a heart
As generous, and as full of noble thoughts,
Lay stricken with the deadliest bolts of grief.
Upon a smooth grey stone sate Roderick there;
The wind above him stirred the hazel boughs,
And murmuring at his feet the river ran.
He sate with folded arms and head declined
Upon his breast, feeding on bitter thoughts,
Till nature gave him in the exhausted sense
Of woe a respite something like repose;
And then the quiet sound of gentle winds
And waters with their lulling consonance
Beguiled him of himself. Of all within
Oblivious there he sate, sentient alone
Of outward nature,—of the whispering leaves
That soothed his ear,—the genial breath of Heaven
That fanned his cheek,—the stream's perpetual flow,
That, with its shadows and its glancing lights,
Dimples and thread-like motions infinite,
For ever varying and yet still the same,
Like time, toward eternity, ran by.
Resting his head upon his master's knees,
Upon the bank beside him Theron lay.

What matters change or state and circumstance,
Or lapse of years, with all their dread events,
To him? What matters it that Roderick wears
The crown no longer, nor the sceptre wields?—
It is the dear-loved hand, whose friendly touch
Had flattered him so oft; it is the voice,
At whose glad summons to the field so oft
From slumber he had started, shaking off
Dreams of the chase, to share the actual joy;
The eye, whose recognition he was wont
To watch and welcome with exultant tongue.

A coming step, unheard by Roderick, roused
His watchful ear, and turning he beheld
Siverian. Father, said the good old man,
As Theron rose and fawned about his knees,
Hast thou some charm, which draws about thee thus
The hearts of all our house,—even to the beast
That lacks discourse of reason, but too oft,
With uncorrupted feeling and dumb faith,
Puts lordly man to shame?—The King replied,
'Tis that mysterious sense by which mankind
To fix their friendships and their loves are led,
And which with fainter influence doth extend
To such poor things as this. As we put off
The cares and passions of this fretful world,
It may be too that we thus far approach
To elder nature, and regain in part
The privilege through sin in Eden lost.
The timid hare soon learns that she may trust
The solitary penitent, and birds
Will light upon the hermit's harmless hand.

Thus Roderick answered in excursive speech,
Thinking to draw the old man's mind from what
Might touch him else too nearly, and himself
Disposed to follow on the lure he threw,
As one whom such imaginations led
Out of the world of his own miseries.
But to regardless ears his words were given,
For on the dog Siverian gazed the while,
Pursuing his own thoughts. Thou hast not felt,

Exclaimed the old man, the earthquake and the
　　storm ;
The kingdom's overthrow, the wreck of Spain,
The ruin of thy royal master's house,
Have reached not thee !—Then turning to the King,
When the destroying enemy drew nigh
Toledo, he continued, and we fled
Before their fury, even while her grief
Was fresh, my mistress would not leave behind
This faithful creature.　Well we knew she thought
Of Roderick then, although she named him not ;
For never since the fatal certainty
Fell on us all, hath that unhappy name,
Save in her prayers, been known to pass her lips
Before this day.　She names him now, and weeps ;
But now her tears are tears of thankfulness,
For blessed hath thy coming been to her
And all who loved the King.
　　　　　　　　His faltering voice
Here failed him, and he paused : recovering soon,
When that poor injured lady, he pursued,
Did in my presence to the Prince absolve
The unhappy King—
　　　　　　　　Absolve him ! Roderick cried,
And in that strong emotion turned his face
Sternly toward Siverian, for the sense
Of shame and self-reproach drove from his mind
All other thoughts.　The good old man replied,
Of human judgments humanly I speak.
Who knows not what Pelayo's life hath been ?
Not happier in all dear domestic ties,
Than worthy for his virtue of the bliss
Which is that virtue's fruit ; and yet did he
Absolve, upon Florinda's tale, the King.
Siverian, thus he said, what most I hoped,
And still within my secret heart believed,
Is now made certain.　Roderick hath been
More sinned against than sinning.　And with that
He clasped his hands, and, lifting them to heaven,
Cried, Would to God that he were yet alive !
For not more gladly did I draw my sword
Against Witiza in our common cause,

Than I would fight beneath his banners now,
And vindicate his name !
                    Did he say this ?
The Prince ? Pelayo ? in astonishment
Roderick exclaimed.—He said it, quoth the old man,
None better knew his kinsman's noble heart,
None loved him better, none bewailed him more :
And as he felt, like me, for his reproach
A deeper grief than for his death, even so
He cherished in his heart the constant thought
Something was yet untold, which, being known,
Would palliate his offence, and make the fall
Of one till then so excellently good,
Less monstrous, less revolting to belief,
More to be pitied, more to be forgiven.

While thus he spake, the fallen King felt his face
Burn, and his blood flow fast.   Down, guilty
            thoughts !
Firmly he said within his soul ; lie still,
Thou heart of flesh !   I thought thou hadst been
            quelled,
And quelled thou shalt be !   Help me, O my God,
That I may crucify this inward foe !
Yea, Thou hast helped me, Father !   I am strong,
O Saviour, in Thy strength.
                    As he breathed thus
His inward supplications, the old man
Eyed him with frequent and unsteady looks.
He had a secret trembling on his lips,
And hesitated, still irresolute
In utterance to embody the dear hope :
Fain would he have it strengthened and assured
By this concording judgment, yet he feared
To have it chilled in cold accoil.   At length
Venturing, he brake with interrupted speech
The troubled silence.   Father Maccabee,
I cannot rest till I have laid my heart
Open before thee.   When Pelayo wished
That his poor kinsman were alive to rear
His banner once again, a sudden thought-
A hope—a fancy—what shall it be called ?

F

Possessed me, that perhaps the wish might see
Its glad accomplishment,—that Roderick lived
And might in glory take the field once more
For Spain.—I see thou startest at the thought !
Yet spurn it not with hasty unbelief,
As though 'twere utterly beyond the scope
Of possible contingency.   I think
That I have calmly satisfied myself
How this is more than idle fancy, more
Than mere imaginations of a mind
Which from its wishes builds a baseless faith.
His horse, his royal robe, his hornéd helm,
His mail and sword were found upon the field ;
But if King Roderick had in battle fallen,
That sword, I know, would only have been found
Clenched in the hand which, living, knew so well
To wield the dreadful steel !   Not in the throng
Confounded, nor amid the torpid stream,
Opening with ignominious arms a way
For flight, would he have perished ! Where the strife
Was hottest, ringed about with slaughtered foes,
Should Roderick have been found : by this sure mark
Ye should have known him, if nought else remained,
That his whole body had been gored with wounds
And quilled with spears, as if the Moors had felt
That in his single life the victory lay,
More than in all the host !
                              Siverian's eyes
Shone with a youthful ardour while he spake,
His gathering brow grew stern, and as he raised
His arm, a warrior's impulse charactered
The impassioned gesture.   But the King was calm,
And heard him with unchanging countenance ;
For he had taken his resolve, and felt
Once more the peace of God within his soul,
As in that hour when by his father's grave
He knelt before Pelayo.
                              Soon the old man
Pursued in calmer tones,—Thus much I dare
Believe, that Roderick fell not on that day
When treason brought about his overthrow.
If yet he live, for sure I think I know

His noble mind, 'tis in some wilderness,
Where, in some savage den inhumed, he drags
The weary load of life, and on his flesh
As on a mortal enemy, inflicts
Fierce vengeance with immitigable hand.
Oh that I knew but where to bend my way
In his dear search ! my voice perhaps might reach
His heart, might reconcile him to himself,
Restore him to his mother ere she dies,
His people and his country : with the sword,
Them and his own good name should he redeem.
Oh, might I but behold him once again
Leading to battle these intrepid bands,
Such as he was,—yea, rising from his fall
More glorious, more beloved ! Soon I believe
Joy would accomplish then what grief hath failed
To do with this old heart, and I should die
Clasping his knees with such intense delight,
That when I woke in heaven, even heaven itself
Could have no higher happiness in store.

Thus fervently he spake, and copious tears
Ran down his cheeks. Full oft the royal Goth,
Since he came forth again among mankind,
Had trembled lest some curious eye should read
His lineaments too closely ; now he longed
To fall upon the neck of that old man,
And give his full heart utterance. But the sense
Of duty, by the pride of self-control
Corroborate, made him steadily repress
His yearning nature. Whether Roderick live,
Paying in penitence the bitter price
Of sin, he answered, or if earth hath given
Rest to his earthly part, is only known
To him and Heaven. Dead is he to the world ;
And let not these imaginations rob
His soul of thy continual prayers, whose aid
Too surely, in whatever world, he needs.
The faithful love that mitigates his fault,
Heavenward addressed, may mitigate his doom.
Living or dead, old man, be sure his soul,—
It were unworthy else,—doth hold with thine

Entire communion ! Doubt not he relies
Firmly on thee, as on a father's love,
Counts on thy offices, and joins with thee
In sympathy and fervent act of faith,
Though regions, or though worlds, should intervene.
Lost as he is, to Roderick this must be
Thy first, best, dearest duty ; next must be
To hold right onward in that noble path,
Which he would counsel, could his voice be heard.
Now therefore aid me, while I call upon
The leaders and the people, that this day
We may acclaim Pelayo for our king.

XVIII.

THE ACCLAMATION.

Now, when from Covadonga, down the vale
Holding his way, the princely mountaineer
Came with that happy family in sight
Of Cangas and his native towers, far off
He saw before the gate, in fair array,
The assembled land. Broad banners were displayed,
And spears were sparkling to the sun, shields shone,
And helmets glittered, and the blaring horn,
With frequent sally of impatient joy,
Provoked the echoes round. Well he areeds,
From yonder ensigns and augmented force,
That Odoar and the Primate from the west
Have brought their aid ; but wherefore all were thus
Instructed as for some great festival,
He found not, till Favila's quicker eye
Catching the ready buckler, the glad boy
Leapt up, and clapping his exultant hands,
Shouted, King ! king ! my father shall be king
This day ! Pelayo started at the word,
And the first thought which smote him brought a sigh
For Roderick's fall ; the second was of hope,
Deliverance for his country, for himself
Enduring fame, and glory for his line.

That high prophetic forethought gathered strength,
As looking to his honoured mate, he read
Her soul's accordant augury ; her eyes
Brightened ; the quickened action of the blood
Tinged with a deeper hue her glowing cheek,
And on her lips there sate a smile which spake
The honourable pride of perfect love,
Rejoicing, for her husband's sake, to share
The lot he chose, the perils he defied,
The lofty fortune which their faith foresaw.

Roderick, in front of all the assembled troops,
Held the broad buckler, following to the end
That steady purpose to the which his zeal
Had this day wrought the chiefs. Tall as himself,
Erect it stood beside him, and his hands
Hung resting on the rim. This was an hour
That sweetened life, repaid and recompensed
All losses ; and although it could not heal
All griefs, yet laid them for a while to rest.
The active agitating joy that filled
The vale, that with contagious influence spread
Through all the exulting mountaineers, that gave
New ardour to all spirits, to all breasts
Inspired fresh impulse of excited hope,
Moved every tongue, and strengthened every limb,—
That joy which every man reflected saw
From every face of all the multitude,
And heard in every voice, in every sound,
Reached not the King. Aloof from sympathy,
He from the solitude of his own soul
Beheld the busy scene. None shared or knew
His deep and incommunicable joy ;
None but that heavenly Father, who alone
Beholds the struggles of the heart, alone
Sees and rewards the secret sacrifice.

Among the chiefs conspicuous, Urban stood,
He whom, with well-weighed choice, in arduous time
To arduous office the consenting Church
Had called when Sindered fear-smitten fled ;
Unfaithful shepherd, who for life alone

Solicitous, forsook his flock, when most
In peril and in suffering they required
A pastor's care.   Far off at Rome he dwells
In ignominious safety, while the Church
Keeps in her annals the deserter's name,
But from the service which with daily zeal
Devout her ancient prelacy recalls,
Blots it, unworthy to partake her prayers.
Urban, to that high station thus being called
From whence disanimating fear had driven
The former primate, for the general weal
Consulting first, removed with timely care
The relics and the written works of saints,
Toledo's choicest treasure, prized beyond
All wealth, their living and their dead remains ;
These to the mountain fastnesses he bore
Of unsubdued Cantabria, there deposed,
One day to be the boast of yet unbuilt
Oviedo, and the dear idolatry
Of multitudes unborn.   To things of state
Then giving thought mature, he held advice
With Odoar, whom of counsel competent
And firm of heart he knew. What then they planned,
Time and the course of over-ruled events
To earlier act had ripened than their hope
Had ever in its gladdest dream proposed ;
And here by agents unforeseen, and means
Beyond the scope of foresight brought about,
This day they saw their dearest heart's desire
Accorded them : all-able Providence
Thus having ordered all, that Spain this hour
With happiest omens, and on surest base,
Should from its ruins rear again her throne.

For acclamation and for sacring now
One form must serve, more solemn for the breach
Of old observances, whose absence here
Deeplier impressed the heart than all display
Of regal pomp and wealth pontifical,
Of vestments radiant with their gems, and stiff
With ornature of gold ; the glittering train,
The long procession, and the full-voiced choir.

This day the forms of piety and war,
In strange but fitting union must combine.
Not in his alb and cope and orary
Came Urban now, nor wore he mitre here,
Precious or auriphrygiate ; bare of head
He stood, all else in arms complete, and o'er
His gorget's iron rings the pall was thrown
Of wool undyed, which on the Apostle's tomb
Gregory had laid, and sanctified with prayer ;
That from the living pontiff and the dead
Replete with holiness it might impart
Doubly derived its grace.   One page beside
Bore his broad-shadowed helm ; another's hand
Held the long spear, more suited in these times
For Urban, than the crosier richly wrought
With silver foliature, the elaborate work
Of Grecian or Italian artist, trained
In the eastern capital, or sacred Rome,
Still o'er the West predominant, though fallen.
Better the spear befits the shepherd's hand
When robbers break the fold.   Now he had laid
The weapon by, and held a natural cross
Of rudest form, unpeeled, even as it grew
On the near oak that morn.
                              Mutilate alike
Of royal rites was this solemnity.
Where was the rubied crown, the sceptre where,
And where the golden pome, the proud array
Of ermines, aureate vests, and jewellery,
With all which Leuvigild for after kings
Left, ostentatious of his power ?   The Moor
Had made his spoil of these, and on the field
Of Xeres, where contending multitudes
Had trampled it beneath their bloody feet,
The standard of the Goths forgotten lay
Defiled, and rotting there in sun and rain.
Utterly is it lost ; nor ever more
Herald or antiquary's patient search
Shall from forgetfulness avail to save
Those blazoned arms, so fatally of old
Renowned through all the affrighted Occident.
That banner, before which imperial Rome

First to a conqueror bowed her head abased ;
Which when the dreadful Hun, with all his powers,
Came like a deluge rolling o'er the world,
Made head, and in the front of battle broke
His force, till then resistless ; which so oft
Had with alternate fortune braved the Frank ;
Driven the Byzantine from the farthest shores
Of Spain, long lingering there, to final flight ;
And of their kingdoms and their name despoiled
The Vandal, and the Alan, and the Sueve ;
Blotted from human records is it now
As it had never been.   So let it rest
With things forgotten !   But Oblivion ne'er
Shall cancel from the historic roll, nor Time,
Who changeth all, obscure that fated sign,
Which brighter now than mountain snows at noon
To the bright sun displays its argent field.

Rose not the vision then upon thy soul,
O Roderick, when within that argent field
Thou saw'st the rampant lion, red as if
Upon some noblest quarry he had rolled,
Rejoicing in his satiate rage, and drunk
With blood and fury ?   Did the auguries
Which opened on thy spirit bring with them
A perilous consolation, deadening heart
And soul, yea, worse than death,—that thou through
      all
Thy chequered way of life, evil and good,
Thy errors and thy virtues, had'st but been
The poor mere instrument of things ordained,—
Doing or suffering, impotent alike
To will or act,—perpetually bemocked
With semblance of volition, yet in all
Blind worker of the ways of destiny !
That thought intolerable, which in the hour
Of woe indignant conscience had repelled,
As little might it find reception now,
When the regenerate spirit self-approved
Beheld its sacrifice complete.   With faith
Elate, he saw the bannered lion float
Refulgent, and recalled that thrilling shout

Which he had heard when on Romano's grave
The joy of victory woke him from his dream,
And sent him with prophetic hope to work
Fulfilment of the great events ordained,
There in imagination's inner world
Prefigured to his soul.

                Alone, advanced
Before the ranks, the Goth in silence stood,
While from all voices round, loquacious joy
Mingled its buzz continuous with the blast
Of horn, shrill pipe, and tinkling cymbals' clash,
And sound of deafening drum.   But when the
    Prince
Drew nigh, and Urban with the cross upheld
Stepped forth to meet him, all at once were stilled
With instantaneous hush ; as when the wind,
Before whose violent gusts the forest oaks,
Tossing like billows their tempestuous heads,
Roar like a raging sea, suspends its force,
And leaves so dead a calm that not a leaf
Moves on the silent spray.   The passing air
Bore with it from the woodland undisturbed
The ringdove s wooing, and the quiet voice
Of waters warbling near.

               Son of a race
Of heroes and of kings ! the Primate thus
Addressed him, thou in whom the Gothic blood,
Mingling with old Iberia's, hath restored
To Spain a ruler of her native line,
Stand forth, and in the face of God and man
Swear to uphold the right, abate the wrong,
With equitable hand, protect the cross
Whereon thy lips this day shall seal their vow,
And underneath that hallowed symbol, wage
Holy and inextinguishable war
Against the accursèd nation that usurps
Thy country's sacred soil !

             So speak of me
Now and for ever, O my countrymen !
Replied Pelayo ; and so deal with me
Here and hereafter, Thou, Almighty God,
In whom I put my trust !

                      F 2

Lord God of Hosts,
Urban pursued, of angels and of men
Creator and Disposer, King of kings,
Ruler of earth and heaven,—look down this day,
And multiply Thy blessings on the head
Of this Thy servant, chosen in Thy sight!
Be Thou his counsellor, his comforter,
His hope, his joy, his refuge and his strength;
Crown him with justice, and with fortitude,
Defend him with Thine all-sufficient shield,
Surround him everywhere with the right hand
Of Thine all-present power, and with the might
Of Thine omnipotence, send in his aid
Thy unseen angels forth, that potently
And royally against all enemies
He may endure and triumph! Bless the land
O'er which he is appointed : bless Thou it
With the waters of the firmament, the springs
Of the low-lying deep, the fruits which sun
And moon mature for man, the precious stores
Of the eternal hills, and all the gifts
Of earth, its wealth and fulness!
                               Then he took
Pelayo's hand, and on his finger placed
The mystic circlet.—With this ring, O Prince,
To our dear Spain, who like a widow now
Mourneth in desolation, I thee wed :
For weal or woe thou takest her, till death
Dispart the union : Be it blest to her,
To thee, and to thy seed!
                               Thus when he ceased,
He gave the awaited signal.   Roderick brought
The buckler: Eight for strength and stature chosen
Came to their honoured office : Round the shield
Standing, they lower it for the chieftain's feet,
Then, slowly raised upon their shoulders, lift
The steady weight.   Erect Pelayo stands,
And thrice he brandishes the burnished sword,
While Urban to the assembled people cries,
Spaniards, behold your King!   The multitude
Then sent forth all their voice with glad acclaim,
Raising the loud *Real;* thrice did the word

Ring through the air, and echo from the walls
Of Cangas.   Far and wide the thundering shout,
Rolling among reduplicating rocks,
Pealed o'er the hills, and up the mountain vales.
The wild ass starting in the forest glade
Ran to the covert ; the affrighted wolf
Skulked through the thicket to a closer brake ;
The sluggish bear, awakened in his den,
Roused up and answered with a sullen growl,
Low-breathed and long ; and at the uproar scared,
The brooding eagle from her nest took wing.

   Heroes and chiefs of old ! and ye who bore
Firm to the last your part in that dread strife,
When Julian and Witiza's viler race
Betrayed their country, hear ye from yon heaven
The joyful acclamation which proclaims
That Spain is born again !   O ye who died
In that disastrous field, and ye who fell
Embracing with a martyr's love your death
Amid the flames of Auria ; and all ye
Victims innumerable, whose cries unheard
On earth, but heard in heaven, from all the land
Went up for vengeance ; not in vain ye cry
Before the eternal throne !—Rest, innocent blood !
Vengeance is due, and vengeance will be given.
Rest, innocent blood ! The appointed age is come !
The star that harbingers a glorious day
Hath risen !   Lo, there the avenger stands !   Lo,
      there
He brandishes the avenging sword !   Lo, there
The avenging banner spreads its argent field
Refulgent with auspicious light !—Rejoice,
O Leon, for thy banner is displayed,
Rejoice with all thy mountains, and thy vales
And streams !   And thou, O Spain, through all thy
      realms,
For thy deliverance cometh !   Even now,
As from all sides the miscreant hosts move on :
From southern Betis ; from the western lands,
Where through redundant vales smooth Minho
      flows,

And Douro pours through vine-clad hills the wealth
Of Leon's gathered waters ; from the plains
Burgensian, in old time Vardulia called,
But in their castellated strength ere long
To be designed Castile, a deathless name ;
From midland regions where Toledo reigns
Proud city on her royal eminence,
And Tagus bends his sickle round the scene
Of Roderick's fall ; from rich Rioja's fields ;
Dark Ebro's shores ; the walls of Salduba,
Seat of the Sedetanians old, by Rome
Cæsarian and August denominate,
Now Zaragoza, in this later time
Above all cities of the earth renowned
For duty perfectly performed ;—east, west
And south, where'er their gathered multitudes
Urged by the speed of vigorous tyranny,
With more than with commensurable strength
Haste to prevent the danger, crush the hopes
Of rising Spain, and rivet round her neck
The eternal yoke,—the ravenous fowls of heaven
Flock there presentient of their food obscene,
Following the accursed armies, whom too well
They know their purveyors long.   Pursue their
    march,
Ominous attendants !   Ere the moon hath filled
Her horns, these purveyors shall become the prey,
And ye on Moorish not on Christian flesh
Wearying your beaks, shall clog your scaly feet
With foreign gore.   Soon will ye learn to know,
Followers and harbingers of blood, the flag
Of Leon where it bids you to your feast !
Terror and flight shall with that flag go forth,
And havoc and the dogs of war and death.
Thou Covadonga with the tainted stream
Of Deva, and this now rejoicing vale,
Soon its primitial triumphs wilt behold !
Nor shall the glories of the noon be less
Than such miraculous promise of the dawn :
Witness Clavijo, where the dreadful cry
Of Santiago, then first heard, o'erpowered
The Akbar, and that holier name blasphemed

By misbelieving lips! Simancas, thou
Be witness! And do ye your record bear,
Tolosan mountains, where the Almohade
Beheld his myriads scattered and destroyed,
Like locusts swept before the stormy North!
Thou too, Salado, on that later day
When Africa received her final foil,
And thy swoln stream incarnadined rolled back
The invaders to the deep,—there shall they toss
Till on their native Mauritanian shore
The waves shall cast their bones to whiten there.

XIX.

RODERICK AND RUSILLA.

WHEN all had been performed, the royal Goth
Looked up toward the chamber in the tower,
Where gazing on the multitude below,
Alone Rusilla stood. He met her eye,
For it was singling him amid the crowd;
Obeying then the hand which beckoned him,
He went with heart prepared, nor shrinking now,
But armed with self-approving thoughts that hour.
Entering in tremulous haste, he closed the door,
And turned to clasp her knees; but lo, she spread
Her arms, and catching him in close embrace,
Fell on his neck, and cried, My son, my son!—
Ere long, controlling that first agony
With effort of strong will, backward she bent,
And gazing on his head now shorn and grey,
And on his furrowed countenance, exclaimed,
Still, still, my Roderick! the same noble mind!
The same heroic heart! Still, still, my son!—
Changed,—yet not wholly fallen,—not wholly lost,
He cried,—not wholly in the sight of Heaven
Unworthy, O my mother, nor in thine!
She locked her arms again around his neck,
Saying, Lord, let me now depart in peace!
And bowed her head again, and silently
Gave way to tears.

                    When that first force was spent,
And passion in exhaustment found relief,—
I knew thee, said Rusilla, when the dog
Rose from my feet, and licked his master's hand.
All flashed upon me then ; the instinctive sense
That goes unerringly where reason fails,—
The voice, the eye,—a mother's thoughts are
    quick,—
Miraculous as it seemed,—Siverian's tale,—
Florinda's,—every action,—every word,—
Each strengthening each, and all confirming all,
Revealed thee, O my son ! but I restrained
My heart, and yielded to thy holier will
The thoughts which rose to tempt a soul not yet
Weaned wholly from the world.
                    What thoughts? replied
Roderick.   That I might see thee yet again
Such as thou wert, she answered ; not alone
To Heaven and me restored, but to thyself,—
Thy crown,—thy country,—all within thy reach ;
Heaven so disposing all things, that the means
Which wrought the ill, might work the remedy.
Methought I saw thee once again the hope,—
The strength,—the pride of Spain !   The miracle
Which I beheld made all things possible.
I know the inconstant people, how their mind,
With every breath of good or ill report,
Fluctuates, like summer corn before the breeze ;
Quick in their hatred, quicker in their love,
Generous and hasty, soon would they redress
All wrongs of former obloquy.—I thought
Of happiness restored,—the broken heart
Healed, — and Count Julian, for his daughter's
    sake,
Turning in thy behalf against the Moors
His powerful sword :—all possibilities
That could be found or fancied, built a dream
Before me ; such as easiest might illude
A lofty spirit trained in palaces,
And not alone amid the flatteries
Of youth with thoughts of high ambition fed
When all is sunshine, but through years of woe,

When sorrow sanctified their use, upheld
By honourable pride and earthly hopes.
I thought I yet might nurse upon my knee
Some young Theodofred, and see in him
Thy father's image and thine own renewed,
And love to think the little hand which there
Played with the bauble, should in after days
Wield the transmitted sceptre ;—that through him
The ancient seed should be perpetuate,—
That precious seed revered so long, desired
So dearly, and so wondrously preserved.

Nay, he replied, Heaven hath not with its bolts
Scathed the proud summit of the tree, and left
The trunk unflawed ; ne'er shall it clothe its boughs
Again, nor push again its scions forth,
Head, root, and branch, all mortified alike !—
Long ere these locks were shorn had I cut off
The thoughts of royalty ! Time might renew
Their growth, as for Manoah's captive son,
And I too on the miscreant race, like him,
Might prove my strength regenerate ; but the hour,
When in its second best nativity,
My soul was born again through grace, this heart
Died to the world. Dreams such as thine pass now
Like evening clouds before me ; if I think
How beautiful they seem, 't is but to feel
How soon they fade, how fast the night shuts in.
But in that world to which my hopes look on,
Time enters not, nor mutability ;
Beauty and goodness are unfading there ;
Whatever there is given us to enjoy,
That we enjoy for ever, still the same.—
Much might Count Julian's sword · achieve for
   Spain
And me, but more will his dear daughter's soul
Effect in heaven ; and soon will she be there
An angel at the throne of grace, to plead
In his behalf and mine.
                    I knew thy heart,
She answered, and subdued the vain desire.
It was the world's last effort. Thou hast chosen

The better part.　Yes, Roderick, even on earth
There is a praise above the monarch's fame,
A higher, holier, more enduring praise,
And this will yet be thine !
　　　　　　　　　Oh, tempt me not,
Mother ! he cried ; nor let ambition take
That specious form to cheat us !　What but this,
Fallen as I am, have I to offer Heaven ?
The ancestral sceptre, public fame, content
Of private life, the general good report,
Power, reputation, happiness,—whate er
The heart of man desires to constitute
His earthly weal,—unerring justice claimed
In forfeiture.　I with submitted soul
Bow to the righteous law and kiss the rod.
Only while thus submitted, suffering thus,—
Only while offering up that name on earth,
Perhaps in trial offered to my choice,
Could I present myself before thy sight ;
Thus only could endure myself, or fix
My thoughts upon that fearful pass, where Death
Stands in the gate of heaven !—Time passes on,
The healing work of sorrow is complete ;
All vain desires have long been weeded out,
All vain regrets subdued ; the heart is dead,
The soul is ripe and eager for her birth.
Bless me, my mother ! and come when it will
The inevitable hour, we die in peace.

So saying, on her knees he bowed his head ;
She raised her hands to heaven and blest her child ;
Then bending forward, as he rose, embraced
And clasped him to her heart, and cried, Once
　　more,
Theodofred, with pride behold thy son !

XX.

THE MOORISH CAMP.

THE times are big with tidings ; every hour
From east and west and south the breathless scouts
Bring swift alarums in ; the gathering foe,
Advancing from all quarters to one point,
Close their wide crescent.   Nor was aid of fear
To magnify their numbers needed now,
They came in myriads.   Africa had poured
Fresh shoals upon the coast of wretched Spain ;
Lured from their hungry deserts to the scene
Of spoil, like vultures to the battle-field,
Fierce, unrelenting, habited in crimes,
Like bidden guests the mirthful ruffians flock
To that free feast which in their Prophet's name
Rapine and lust proclaimed.   Nor were the chiefs
Of victory less assured, by long success
Elate, and proud of that o'erwhelming strength,
Which, surely they believed, as it had rolled
Thus far unchecked would roll victorious on,
Till, like the Orient, the subjected West
Should bow in reverence at Mahommed's name,
And pilgrims, from remotest Arctic shores,
Tread with religious feet the burning sands
Of Araby, and Mecca's stony soil.
Proud of his part in Roderick's overthrow,
Their leader Abulcacem came, a man
Immitigable, long in war renowned.
Here Magued comes, who on the conquered walls
Of Cordoba, by treacherous fear betrayed,
Planted the moony standard : Ibrahim here,
He, who by Genil and in Darro's vales,
Had for the Moors the fairest portion won
Of all their spoils, fairest and best maintained,
And to the Alpuxarras given in trust
His other name, through them preserved in song.
Here too, Alcahman, vaunting his late deeds
At Auria, all her children by the sword
Cut off, her bulwarks rased, her towers laid low,
Her dwellings by devouring flames consumed,

Bloody and hard of heart, he little weened,
Vain-boastful chief ! that from those fatal flames
The fire of retribution had gone forth
Which soon should wrap him round.
                      The renegades
Here too were seen, Ebba and Sisibert ;
A spurious brood, but of their parent's crimes
True heirs, in guilt begotten, and in ill
Trained up. The same unnatural rage that turned
Their swords against their country, made them seek,
Unmindful of their wretched mother's end,
Pelayo's life. No enmity is like
Domestic hatred. For his blood they thirst,
As if that sacrifice might satisfy
Witiza's guilty ghost, efface the shame
Of their adulterous birth, and one crime more
Crowning a hideous course, emancipate
Thenceforth their spirits from all earthly fear.
This was their only care ; but other thoughts
Were rankling in that elder villain's mind,
Their kinsman Orpas, he of all the crew
Who in this fatal visitation fell,
The foulest and the falsest wretch that e'er
Renounced his baptism. From his cherished views
Of royalty cut off, he coveted
Count Julian's wide domains, and hopeless now
To gain them through the daughter, laid his toils
Against the father's life,—the instrument
Of his ambition first, and now designed
Its victim. To this end with cautious hints,
At favouring season ventured, he possessed
The leader's mind ; then, subtly fostering
The doubts himself had sown, with bolder charge
He bade him warily regard the Count,
Lest underneath an outward show of faith
The heart uncircumcised were Christian still :
Else, wherefore had Florinda not obeyed
Her dear loved sire's example, and embraced
The saving truth ? Else, wherefore was her hand,
Plighted to him so long, so long withheld,
Till she had found a fitting hour to fly
With that audacious Prince, who now in arms,

Defied the Caliph's power ;—for who could doubt
That in his company she fled, perhaps
The mover of his flight ?   What if the Count
Himself had planned the evasion which he feigned
In sorrow to condemn ?   What if she went
A pledge assured, to tell the mountaineers
That when they met the Mussulmans in the heat
Of fight, her father passing to their side
Would draw the victory with him ?—Thus he
    breathed
Fiend-like in Abulcacem's ear his schemes
Of murderous malice ; and the course of things,
Ere long, in part approving his discourse,
Aided his aim, and gave his wishes weight.
For scarce on the Asturian territory
Had they set foot, when, with the speed of fear,
Count Eudon, nothing doubting that their force
Would like a flood sweep all resistance down,
Hastened to plead his merits ;—he alone,
Found faithful in obedience through reproach
And danger, when the maddened multitude
Hurried their chiefs along, and high and low
With one infectious frenzy seized, provoked
The invincible in arms.   Pelayo led
The raging crew,—he doubtless the prime spring
Of all these perilous movements ; and 'twas said
He brought the assurance of a strong support,
Count Julian's aid, for in his company
From Cordoba, Count Julian's daughter came.

Thus Eudon spake before the assembled chiefs ;
When instantly a stern and wrathful voice
Replied, I know Pelayo never made
That senseless promise !   He who raised the tale
Lies foully ; but the bitterest enemy
That ever hunted for Pelayo's life
Hath never with the charge of falsehood touched
His name.
        The Baron had not recognised
Till then, beneath the turban's shadowing folds,
Julian's swart visage, where the fiery skies
Of Africa, through many a year's long course,

Had set their hue inburnt.   Something he sought
In quick excuse to say of common fame,
Lightly believed and busily diffused,
And that no enmity had moved his speech
Repeating rumour's tale.   Julian replied,
Count Eudon, neither for thyself nor me
Excuse is needed here.   The path I tread
Is one wherein there can be no return,
No pause, no looking back !   A choice like mine
For time and for eternity is made,
Once and for ever ! and as easily
The breath of vain report might build again
The throne which my just vengeance overthrew,
As in the Caliph and his captain's mind
Affect the opinion of my well-tried truth.
The tidings which thou givest me of my child
Touch me more vitally ; bad though they be,
A secret apprehension of aught worse
Makes me with joy receive them.
                              Then the Count
To Abulcacem turned his speech, and said,
I pray thee, chief, give me a messenger
By whom I may to this unhappy child
Despatch a father's bidding, such as yet
May win her back.   What I would say requires
No veil of privacy ; before ye all
The errand shall be given.
                              Boldly he spake,
Yet wary in that show of open truth,
For well he knew what dangers girt him round
Amid the faithless race.   Blind with revenge,
For them in madness had he sacrificed
His name, his baptism, and his native land,
To feel, still powerful as he was, that life
Hung on their jealous favour.   But his heart
Approved him now, where love, too long restrained,
Resumed its healing influence, leading him
Right on with no misgiving.   Chiefs, he said,
Hear me, and let your wisdom judge between
Me and Prince Orpas !—Known it is to all,
Too well; what mortal injury provoked
My spirit to that vengeance which your aid

So signally hath given. A covenant
We made when first our purpose we combined,
That he should have Florinda for his wife,
My only child, so should she be, I thought,
Revenged and honoured best. My word was
    given
Truly, nor did I cease to use all means
Of counsel or command, entreating her
Sometimes with tears, seeking sometimes with threats
Of an offended father's curse to enforce
Obedience ; that, she said, the Christian law
Forbade, moreover she had vowed herself
A servant to the Lord. In vain I strove
To win her to the Prophet's saving faith,
Using perhaps a rigour to that end
Beyond permitted means, and to my heart,
Which loved her dearer than its own life-blood,
Abhorrent. Silently she suffered all,
Or when I urged her with most vehemence,
Only replied, I knew her fixed resolve,
And craved my patience but a little while
Till death should set her free. Touched as I
    was,
I yet persisted, till at length to escape
The ceaseless importunity, she fled :
And verily I feared until this hour,
My rigour to some fearfuller resolve
Than flight, had driven my child. Chiefs, I appeal
To each and all, and Orpas to thyself
Especially, if, having thus essayed
All means that law and nature have allowed
To bend her will, I may not rightfully
Hold myself free, that promise being void
Which cannot be fulfilled ?
                Thou sayest then,
Orpas replied, that from her false belief
Her stubborn opposition drew its force.
I should have thought that from the ways corrupt
Of these idolatrous Christians, little care
Might have sufficed to wean a duteous child,
The example of a parent so beloved
Leading the way ; and yet I will not doubt

Thou didst enforce with all sincerity
And holy zeal upon thy daughter's mind
The truths of Islam.
           Julian knit his brow,
And scowling on the insidious renegade,
He answered, By what reasoning my poor mind
Was from the old idolatry reclaimed,
None better knows than Seville's mitred chief,
Who first renouncing errors which he taught,
Led me his follower to the Prophet's pale.
Thy lessons I repeated as I could ;
Of graven images, unnatural vows,
False records, fabling creeds, and juggling priests,
Who making sanctity the cloak of sin,
Laughed at the fools on whose credulity
They fattened.   To these arguments, whose worth
Prince Orpas, least of all men, should impeach,
I added, like a soldier bred in arms,
And to the subtleties of schools unused,
The flagrant fact, that Heaven with victory,
Where'er they turned, attested and approved
The chosen Prophet's arms.   If thou wert still
The mitred Metropolitan, and I
Some wretch of Arian or of Hebrew race,
Thy proper business then might be to pry,
And question me for lurking flaws of faith.
We Mussulmans, Prince Orpas, live beneath
A wiser law, which with the iniquities
Of thine old craft, hath abrogated this,
Its foulest practice!
           As Count Julian ceased,
From underneath his black and gathered brow
There went a look, which with these wary words
Bore to the heart of that false renegade
Their whole envenomed meaning.   Haughtily
Withdrawing then his altered eyes, he said,
Too much of this ! return we to the sum
Of my discourse.   Let Abulcacem say,
In whom the Caliph speaks, if with all faith
Having essayed in vain all means to win
My child's consent, I may not hold henceforth
The covenant discharged.

The Moor replied,
Well hast thou said, and rightly may'st assure
Thy daughter that the Prophet's holy law
Forbids compulsion.   Give thine errand now ;
The messenger is here.
                    Then Julian said,
Go to Pelayo, and from him entreat
Admittance to my child, where'er she be.
Say to her, that her father solemnly
Annuls the covenant with Orpas pledged,
Nor with solicitations, nor with threats,
Will urge her more, nor from that liberty
Of faith restrain her, which the Prophet's law,
Liberal as heaven from whence it came, to all
Indulges.   Tell her that her father says
His days are numbered, and beseeches her
By that dear love, which from her infancy
Still he hath borne her, growing as she grew,
Nursed in our weal and strengthened in our woe,
She will not in the evening of his life
Leave him forsaken and alone.   Enough
Of sorrow, tell her, have her injuries
Brought on her father's head ; let not her act
Thus aggravate the burden.   Tell her too,
That when he prayed her to return, he wept
Profusely as a child ; but bitterer tears
Than ever fell from childhood's eyes, were those
Which traced his hardy cheeks.
                          With faltering voice
He spake, and after he had ceased from speech
His lip was quivering still.   The Moorish chief
Then to the messenger his bidding gave.
Say, cried he, to these rebel infidels,
Thus Abulcacem in the Caliph's name
Exhorteth them : Repent and be forgiven !
Nor think to stop the dreadful storm of war,
Which conquering and to conquer must fulfil
Its destined circle, rolling eastward now
Back from the subjugated west, to sweep
Thrones and dominions down, till in the bond
Of unity all nations join, and earth
Acknowledge, as she sees one sun in heaven,

One God, one chief, one Prophet, and one law.
Jerusalem, the holy city, bows
To holier Mecca's creed ; the crescent shines
Triumphant o'er the eternal pyramids ;
On the cold altars of the worshippers
Of fire, moss grows, and reptiles leave their slime ;
The African idolatries are fallen,
And Europe's senseless gods of stone and wood
Have had their day.   Tell these misguided men,
A moment for repentance yet is left,
And mercy the submitted neck will spare
Before the sword is drawn : but once unsheathed,
Let Auria witness how that dreadful sword
Accomplisheth its work ! They little know
The Moors who hope in battle to withstand
Their valour, or in flight escape their rage !
Amid our deserts we hunt down the birds
Of heaven,—wings do not save them ! Nor shall
        rocks,
And holds, and fastnesses, avail to save
These mountaineers.   Is not the earth the Lord's ?
And we, His chosen people, whom He sends
To conquer and possess it in His name ?

XXI.

THE FOUNTAIN IN THE FOREST.

THE second eve had closed upon their march
Within the Asturian border, and the Moors
Had pitched their tents amid an open wood
Upon the mountain side.   As day grew dim,
Their scattered fires shone with distincter light
Among the trees, above whose top the smoke
Diffused itself, and stained the evening sky.
Ere long the stir of occupation ceased,
And all the murmur of the busy host
Subsiding died away, as through the camp
The crier from a knoll proclaimed the hour
For prayer appointed, and with sonorous voice,

Thrice in melodious modulation full,
Pronounced the highest name.   There is no God
But God, he cried ; there is no God but God !
Mahommed is the Prophet of the Lord !
Come ye to prayer ! to prayer ! The Lord is great !
There is no God but God !—Thus he pronounced
His ritual form, mingling with holiest truth
The audacious name accursed.   The multitude
Made their ablutions in the mountain stream
Obedient, then their faces to the earth
Bent in formality of easy prayer.

   An arrow's flight above that mountain stream
There was a little glade, where underneath
A long smooth mossy stone a fountain rose.
An oak grew near, and with its ample boughs
O'ercanopied the spring ; its fretted roots
Embossed the bank, and on their tufted bark
Grew plants which love the moisture and the shade ;
Short ferns, and longer leaves of wrinkled green
Which bent toward the spring, and when the wind
Made itself felt, just touched with gentle dip
The glassy surface, ruffled ne'er but then,
Save when a bubble rising from the depth
Burst, and with faintest circles marked its place,
Or if an insect skimmed it with its wing,
Or when in heavier drops the gathered rain
Fell from the oak's high bower.   The mountain roe,
When, having drank there, he would bound across,
Drew up upon the bank his meeting feet,
And put forth half his force.   With silent lapse
From thence through mossy banks the water stole,
Then murmuring hastened to the glen below.
Diana might have loved in that sweet spot
To take her noontide rest ; and when she stooped
Hot from the chase to drink, well pleased had seen
Her own bright crescent, and the brighter face
It crowned, reflected there.
               Beside that spring
Count Julian's tent was pitched upon the glade ;
There his ablutions Moor-like he performed,
And Moor-like knelt in prayer, bowing his head

G

Upon the mossy bank. There was a sound
Of voices at the tent when he arose,
And lo! with hurried step a woman came
Toward him; rightly then his heart presaged,
And ere he could behold her countenance,
Florinda knelt, and with uplifted arms
Embraced her sire. He raised her from the ground,
Kissed her, and clasped her to his heart, and said,
Thou hast not then forsaken me, my child!
Howe'er the inexorable will of Fate
May in the world which is to come divide
Our everlasting destinies, in this
Thou wilt not, O my child, abandon me!
And then with deep and interrupted voice,
Nor seeking to restrain his copious tears,
My blessing be upon thy head, he cried,
A father's blessing! Though all faiths were false,
It should not lose its worth!—She locked her hands
Around his neck, and gazing in his face
Through streaming tears, exclaimed, Oh, nevermore,
Here or hereafter, never let us part!
And breathing then a prayer in silence forth,
The name of Jesus trembled on her tongue.

Whom hast thou there? cried Julian, and drew
  back,
Seeing that near them stood a meagre man
In humble garb, who rested with raised hands
On a long staff, bending his head like one
Who when he hears the distant vesper-bell,
Halts by the way, and, all unseen of men,
Offers his homage in the eye of Heaven.
She answered, Let not my dear father frown
In anger on his child! Thy messenger
Told me that I should be restrained no more
From liberty of faith, which the new law
Indulged to all; how soon my hour might come
I knew not, and although that hour will bring
Few terrors, yet methinks I would not be
Without a Christian comforter in death.

A priest! exclaimed the Count, and drawing back,
Stooped for his turban, that he might not lack

Some outward symbol of apostacy;
For still in war his wonted arms he wore,
Nor for the scimitar had changed the sword
Accustomed to his hand.   He covered now
His short grey hair, and under the white folds
His swarthy brow, which gathered as he rose,
Darkened.   Oh, frown not thus! Florinda said;
A kind and gentle counsellor is this,
One who pours balm into a wounded soul,
And mitigates the griefs he cannot heal.
I told him I had vowed to pass my days
A servant of the Lord, yet that my heart,
Hearing the message of thy love, was drawn
With powerful yearnings back. Follow thy heart,—
It answers to the call of duty here,
He said, nor canst thou better serve the Lord
Than at thy father's side.
     Count Julian's brow,
While thus she spake, insensibly relaxed.
A priest, cried he, and thus with even hand
Weigh vows and natural duty in the scale?
In what old heresy hath he been trained?
Or in what wilderness hath he escaped
The domineering Prelate's fire and sword?
Come hither, man, and tell me who thou art!

 A sinner, Roderick, drawing nigh, replied;
Brought to repentance by the grace of God,
And trusting for forgiveness through the blood
Of Christ in humble hope.
     A smile of scorn
Julian assumed, but merely from the lips
It came; for he was troubled while he gazed
On the strong countenance and thoughtful eye
Before him.   A new law hath been proclaimed,
Said he, which overthrows in its career
The Christian altars of idolatry.
What think'st thou of the Prophet?—Roderick
Made answer, I am in the Moorish camp,
And he who asketh is a Mussulman.
How then should I reply?—Safely, rejoined
The renegade, and freely may'st thou speak

To all that Julian asks.   Is not the yoke
Of Mecca easy, and its burden light?—
Spain hath not found it so, the Goth replied,
And groaning, turned away his countenance.

Count Julian knit his brow, and stood a while
Regarding him with meditative eye
In silence.   Thou art honest too, he cried ;
Why 'twas in quest of such a man as this
That the old Grecian searched by lantern light
In open day the city's crowded streets,
So rare he deemed the virtue.   Honesty
And sense of natural duty in a priest !
Now for a miracle, ye saints of Spain !
I shall not pry too closely for the wires,
For, seeing what I see, ye have me now
In the believing mood !
                              O blessed saints,
Florinda cried, 'tis from the bitterness,
Not from the hardness of the heart, he speaks !
Hear him ! and in your goodness give the scoff
The virtue of a prayer !   So saying, she raised
Her hands in fervent action clasped to heaven :
Then as, still clasped, they fell, toward her sire
She turned her eyes, beholding him through tears.
The look, the gesture, and that silent woe,
Softened her father's heart, which in this hour
Was open to the influences of love.
Priest, thy vocation were a blessed one,
Said Julian, if its mighty power were used
To lessen human misery, not to swell
The mournful sum, already all too great.
If, as thy former counsel should imply,
Thou art not one who would for his craft's sake
Fret with corrosives and inflame the wound
Which the poor sufferer brings to thee in trust
That thou with virtuous balm will bind it up,—
If, as I think, thou art not one of those
Whose villainy makes honest men turn Moors,
Thou then wilt answer with unbiassed mind
What I shall ask thee, and exorcise thus
The sick and feverish conscience of my child,

From inbred phantoms, fiend-like, which possess
Her innocent spirit.   Children we are all
Of one great Father, in whatever clime
Nature or chance hath cast the seeds of life,
All tongues, all colours : neither after death
Shall we be sorted into languages
And tints,—white, black, and tawny, Greek and
    Goth,
Northmen and offspring of hot Africa ;
The All-Father, He in whom we live and move,
He, the indifferent Judge of all, regards
Nations, and hues, and dialects alike ;
According to their works shall they be judged,
When even-handed Justice in the scale
Their good and evil weighs.   All creeds, I ween,
Agree in this, and hold it orthodox.

   Roderick, perceiving here that Julian paused,
As if he waited for acknowledgment
Of that plain truth, in motion of assent
Inclined his brow complacently, and said,
Even so: What follows?   This, resumed the
    Count ;
That creeds like colours being but accident,
Are therefore in the scale imponderable ;—
Thou seest my meaning ?—that from every faith
As every clime, there is a way to heaven,
And thou and I may meet in Paradise.

   Oh, grant it, God ! cried Roderick fervently,
And smote his breast.   Oh, grant it, gracious God !
Through the dear blood of Jesus, grant that he
And I may meet before the mercy throne !
That were a triumph of redeeming love,
For which admiring angels would renew
Their hallelujahs through the choir of heaven !
Man ! quoth Count Julian, wherefore art thou
    moved
To this strange passion?   I require of thee
Thy judgment, not thy prayers !
                        Be not displeased !
In gentle voice subdued the Goth replies ;

A prayer, from whatsoever lips it flow,
By thine own rule should find the way to heaven,
So that the heart in its sincerity
Straight forward breathe it forth.   I, like thyself,
Am all untrained to subtleties of speech,
Nor competent of this great argument
Thou openest ; and perhaps shall answer thee
Wide of the words, but to the purport home.
There are to whom the light of gospel truth
Hath never reached ; of such I needs must deem
As of the sons of men who had their day
Before the light was given.   But, Count, for those
Who, born amid the light, to darkness turn
Wilful in error,—I dare only say,
God doth not leave the unhappy soul without
An inward monitor, and till the grave
Open, the gate of mercy is not closed.

      Priest-like ! the renegade replied, and shook
His head in scorn.   What is not in the craft
Is error, and for error there shall be
No mercy found in Him whom yet ye name
The Merciful !
                    Now God forbid, rejoined
The fallen King, that one who stands in need
Of mercy for his sins should argue thus
Of error !   Thou hast said that thou and I,
Thou dying in name a Mussulman, and I
A servant of the Cross, may meet in heaven,
Time was when in our fathers' ways we walked
Regardlessly alike ; faith being to each,—
For so far thou hast reasoned rightly,—like
Our country's fashion and our mother tongue,
Of mere inheritance,—no thing of choice
In judgment fixed, nor rooted in the heart.
Me have the arrows of calamity
Sore stricken ; sinking underneath the weight
Of sorrow, yet more heavily oppressed
Beneath the burthen of my sins, I turned
In that dread hour to Him who from the Cross
Calls to the heavy laden.   There I found
Relief and comfort ; there I have my hope,

My strength and my salvation ; there, the grave
Ready beneath my feet, and heaven in view
I to the King of Terrors say, Come, Death,—
Come quickly ! Thou too wert a stricken deer,
Julian,—God pardon the unhappy hand
That wounded thee !—but whither didst thou go
For healing ? Thou hast turned away from Him,
Who saith, Forgive as ye would be forgiven ;
And that the Moorish sword might do thy work,
Received the creed of Mecca : with what fruit
For Spain, let tell her cities sacked, her sons
Slaughtered, her daughters than thine own dear
    child
More foully wronged, more wretched ! For thyself,
Thou hast had thy fill of vengeance, and perhaps
The cup was sweet : but it hath left behind
A bitter relish ! Gladly would thy soul
Forget the past ; as little canst thou bear
To send into futurity thy thoughts :
And for this Now, what is it, Count, but fear—
However bravely thou mayest bear thy front,—
Danger, remorse, and stinging obloquy?
One only hope, one only remedy,
One only refuge yet remains—My life
Is at thy mercy, Count ! Call, if thou wilt,
Thy men, and to the Moors deliver me !
Or strike thyself ! Death were from any hand
A welcome gift ; from thine, and in this cause,
A boon indeed ! My latest words on earth
Should tell thee that all sins may be effaced,
Bid thee repent, have faith, and be forgiven !
Strike, Julian, if thou wilt, and send my soul
To intercede for thine, that we may meet,
Thou and thy child and I, beyond the grave.

Thus Roderick spake, and spread his arms as if
He offered to the sword his willing breast,
With looks of passionate persuasion fixed
Upon the Count, who in his first access
Of anger, seemed as though he would have called
His guards to seize the priest. The attitude
Disarmed him, and that fervent zeal sincere,

And more than both, the look and voice, which like
A mystery troubled him.   Florinda too
Hung on his arm with both her hands, and cried,
O father, wrong him not ! he speaks from God !
Life and salvation are upon his tongue !
Judge thou the value of that faith whereby,
Reflecting on the past, I murmur not,
And to the end of all look on with joy
Of hope assured !
                Peace, innocent ! replied
The Count, and from her hold withdrew his arm.
Then with a gathered brow of mournfulness
Rather than wrath, regarding Roderick, said,
Thou preachest that all sins may be effaced :
Is there forgiveness, Christian, in thy creed
For Roderick's crime ?—For Roderick and for thee,
Count Julian, said the Goth, and as he spake
Trembled through every fibre of his frame,
The gate of heaven is open.   Julian threw
His wrathful hand aloft, and cried, Away !
Earth could not hold us both, nor can one heaven
Contain my deadliest enemy and me !

   My father, say not thus ! Florinda cried ;
I have forgiven him ! I have prayed for him !
For him, for thee, and for myself I pour
One constant prayer to Heaven ! In passion then
She knelt, and bending back, with arms and face
Raised toward the sky, the supplicant exclaimed,
Redeemer, heal his heart ! It is the grief
Which festers there that hath bewildered him !
Save him, Redeemer ! by Thy precious death
Save, save him, O my God ! Then on her face
She fell, and thus with bitterness pursued
In silent throes her agonising prayer.

   Afflict not thus thyself, my child, the Count
Exclaimed ; O dearest, be thou comforted ;
Set but thy heart at rest, I ask no more !
Peace, dearest, peace !—and weeping as he spake,
He knelt to raise her.   Roderick also knelt ;
Be comforted, he cried, and rest in faith

That God will hear thy prayers! they must be heard.
He who could doubt the worth of prayers like thine
May doubt of all things! Sainted as thou art
In sufferings here, this miracle will be
Thy work and thy reward !
               Then raising her,
They seated her upon the fountain's brink,
And there beside her sate.   The moon had risen,
And that fair spring lay blackened half in shade,
Half like a burnished mirror in her light.
By that reflected light Count Julian saw
That Roderick's face was bathed with tears, and pale
As monumental marble.   Friend, said he,
Whether thy faith be fabulous, or sent
Indeed from Heaven, its dearest gift to man,
Thy heart is true : and had the mitred priest
Of Seville been like thee, or hadst thou held
The place he filled ;—but this is idle talk,—
Things are as they will be ; and we, poor slaves,
Fret in the harness as we may, must drag
The car of Destiny where'er she drives,
Inexorable and blind !
              Oh, wretched man,
Cried Roderick, if thou seekest to assuage
Thy wounded spirit with that deadly drug,
Hell's subtlest venom ; look to thine own heart,
Where thou hast will and conscience to belie
This juggling sophistry, and lead thee yet
Through penitence to Heaven !
               Whate'er it be
That governs us, in mournful tone the Count
Replied, Fate, Providence, or Allah's will,
Or reckless Fortune, still the effect the same,
A world of evil and of misery !
Look where we will we meet it ; wheresoe'er
We go we bear it with us.   Here we sit
Upon the margin of this peaceful spring,
And oh ! what volumes of calamity
Would be unfolded here, if either heart
Laid open its sad records !   Tell me not
Of goodness !   Either in some freak of power
This frame of things was fashioned, then cast off

                          G 2

To take its own wild course, the sport of chance :
Or the bad spirit o'er the good prevails,
And in the eternal conflict hath arisen
Lord of the ascendant !

                            Rightly wouldst thou say
Were there no world but this ! the Goth replied.
The happiest child of earth that e'er was marked
To be the minion of prosperity,
Richest in corporal gifts and wealth of mind,
Honour and fame attending him abroad,
Peace and all dear domestic joys at home,
And sunshine till the evening of his days
Closed in without a cloud,—even such a man
Would from the gloom and horror of his heart
Confirm thy fatal thought, were this world all.
Oh ! who could bear the haunting mystery,
If death and retribution did not solve
The riddle, and to heavenliest harmony
Reduce the seeming chaos !—Here we see
The water at its well-head ; clear it is,
Not more transpicuous the invisible air ;
Pure as an infant's thoughts ; and here to life
And good directed all its uses serve.
The herb grows greener on its brink ; sweet flowers
Bend o'er the stream that feeds their freshened roots;
The red-breast loves it for his wintry haunts ;
And when the buds begin to open forth,
Builds near it with his mate their brooding nest ;
The thirsty stag with widening nostrils there
Invigorated draws his copious draught ;
And there amid its flags the wild-boar stands,
Nor suffering wrong nor meditating hurt.
Through woodlands and through solitary fields
Unsullied thus it holds its bounteous course ;
But when it reaches the resorts of men,
The service of the city there defiles
The tainted stream ; corrupt and foul it flows
Through loathsome banks and o'er a bed impure,
Till in the sea, the appointed end to which
Through all its way it hastens, 'tis received,
And, losing all pollution, mingles there
In the wide world of waters. So is it

With the great stream of things, if all were seen ;
Good the beginning, good the end shall be,
And transitory evil only make
The good end happier.　Ages pass away
Thrones fall, and nations disappear, and worlds
Grow old and go to wreck ; the soul alone
Endures, and what she chooseth for herself,
The arbiter of her own destiny,
That only shall be permanent.
　　　　　　　　　　　　But guilt,
And all our suffering ? said the Count.　The Goth
Replied, Repentance taketh sin away,
Death remedies the rest.—Soothed by the strain
Of such discourse, Julian was silent then,
And sate contemplating.　Florinda too
Was calmed : If sore experience may be thought
To teach the uses of adversity,
She said, alas ! who better learned than I
In that sad school !　Methinks, if ye would know
How visitations of calamity
Affect the pious soul, 'tis shown ye there !
Look yonder at that cloud, which through the sky
Sailing alone, doth cross in her career
The rolling moon !　I watched it as it came,
And deemed the deep opaque would blot her beams
But, melting like a wreath of snow, it hangs
In folds of wavy silver round, and clothes
The orb with richer beauties than her own,
Then passing, leaves her in her light serene.

　　Thus having said, the pious sufferer sate,
Beholding with fixed eyes that lovely orb,
Till quiet tears confused in dizzy light
The broken moonbeams.　They too by the toil
Of spirit, as by travail of the day
Subdued, were silent, yielding to the hour.
The silver cloud diffusing slowly past,
And now into its airy elements
Resolved is gone ; while through the azure depth
Alone in Heaven the glorious moon pursues
Her course appointed, with indifferent beams
Shining upon the silent hills around,

And the dark tents of that unholy host,
Who, all unconscious of impending fate,
Take their last slumber there.   The camp is still ;
The fires have mouldered, and the breeze which stirs
The soft and snowy embers, just lays bare
At times a red and evanescent light,
Or for a moment wakes a feeble flame.
They by the fountain hear the stream below,
Whose murmurs, as the wind arose or fell,
Fuller or fainter reach the ear attuned.
And now the nightingale, not distant far,
Began her solitary song ; and poured
To the cold moon a richer, stronger strain
Than that with which the lyric lark salutes
The new-born day.   Her deep and thrilling song
Seemed with its piercing melody to reach
The soul, and in mysterious unison
Blend with all thoughts of gentleness and love.
Their hearts were open to the healing power
Of nature ; and the splendour of the night,
The flow of waters, and that sweetest lay
Came to them like a copious evening dew
Falling on vernal herbs which thirst for rain.

XXII.

THE MOORISH COUNCIL.

THUS they beside the fountain sate, of food
And rest forgetful, when a messenger
Summoned Count Julian to the leader's tent.
In council there at that late hour he found
The assembled chiefs, on sudden tidings called
Of unexpected weight from Cordoba.
Jealous that Abdalazis had assumed
A regal state, affecting in his court
The forms of Gothic sovereignty, the Moors,
Whom artful spirits of ambitious mould
Stirred up, had risen against him in revolt :
And he who late had in the Caliph's name

Ruled from the ocean to the Pyrenees,
A mutilate and headless carcass now,
From pitying hands received beside the road
A hasty grave, scarce hidden there from dogs
And ravens, nor from wintry rains secure.
She, too, who in the wreck of Spain preserved
Her queenly rank, the wife of Roderick first,
Of Abdalazis after, and to both
Alike unhappy, shared the ruin now
Her counsels had brought on ; for she had led
The infatuate Moor, in dangerous vauntery,
To these aspiring forms,—so should he gain
Respect and honour from the Mussulmans,
She said, and that the obedience of the Goths
Followed the sceptre.   In an evil hour
She gave the counsel, and in evil hour
He lent a willing ear ; the popular rage
Fell on them both ; and they to whom her name
Had been a mark for mockery and reproach,
Shuddered with human horror at her fate.
Ayub was heading the wild anarchy ;
But where the cement of authority
Is wanting, all things there are dislocate :
The mutinous soldiery, by every cry
Of rumour set in wild career, were driven
By every gust of passion, setting up
One hour, what in the impulse of the next,
Equally unreasoning, they destroyed : thus all
Was in misrule where uproar gave the law,
And ere from far Damascus they could learn
The Caliph's pleasure, many a moon must pass.
What should be done ? should Abulcacem march
To Cordoba, and in the Caliph's name
Assume the power which to his rank in arms
Rightly devolved, restoring thus the reign
Of order ? or pursue with quickened speed
The end of this great armament, and crush
Rebellion first, then to domestic ills
Apply his undivided mind and force
Victorious ?   What in this emergency
Was Julian's counsel, Abulcacem asked ;
Should they accomplish soon their enterprise ?

Or would the insurgent infidels prolong
The contest, seeking by protracted war
To weary them, and trusting in the strength
Of these wild hills?

                    Julian replied, The chief
Of this revolt is wary, resolute,
Of approved worth in war : a desperate part
He for himself deliberately hath chosen,
Confiding in the hereditary love
Borne to him by these hardy mountaineers,
A love which his own noble qualities
Have strengthened so that every heart is his.
When ye can bring them to the open proof
Of battle, ye will find them in his cause
Lavish of life ; but well they know the strength
Of their own fastnesses, the mountain paths
Impervious to pursuit, the vantages
Of rock, and pass, and woodland, and ravine ;
And hardly will ye tempt them to forego.
These natural aids wherein they put their trust
As in their stubborn spirit, each alike
Deemed by themselves invincible, and so
By Roman found and Goth—beneath whose sway
Slowly persuaded rather than subdued
They came, and still through every change retained
Their manners obstinate and barbarous speech.
My counsel, therefore, is that we secure
With strong increase of force the adjacent posts,
And chiefly Gegio, leaving them so manned
As may abate the hope of enterprise,
Their strength being told.   Time in a strife like this
Becomes the ally of those who trust in him :
Make then with Time your covenant.   Old feuds
May disunite the chiefs : some may be gained
By fair entreaty, others by the stroke
Of nature, or of policy, cut off.
This was the counsel which in Cordoba
I offered Abdalazis : in ill hour
Rejecting it, he sent upon this war
His father's faithful friend ! Dark are the ways
Of destiny ! had I been at his side
Old Muza would not now have mourned his age

Left childless, nor had Ayub dared defy
The Caliph's represented power. The case
Calls for thine instant presence, with the weight
Of thy legitimate authority.

Julian, said Orpas, turning from beneath
His turban to the Count a crafty eye,
Thy daughter is returned ; doth she not bring
Some tidings of the movements of the foe ?
The Count replied, When child and parent meet,
First reconciled from discontents which wrung
The hearts of both, ill should their converse be
Of warlike matters ! There hath been no time
For such inquiries, neither should I think
To ask her touching that for which I know
She hath neither eye nor thought.
                                        There was a time,
Orpas with smile malignant thus replied,
When in the progress of the Caliph's arms
Count Julian's daughter had an interest
Which touched her nearly ! But her turn is served,
And hatred of Prince Orpas may beget
Indifference to the cause. Yet Destiny
Still guideth to the service of the faith
The wayward heart of woman ; for as one
Delivered Roderick to the avenging sword,
So hath another at this hour betrayed
Pelayo to his fall. His sister came
At nightfall to my tent a fugitive.
She tells me that on learning our approach
The rebel to a cavern in the hills
Had sent his wife and children, and with them
Those of his followers, thinking there concealed
They might be safe. She, moved by injuries
Which stung her spirit, on the way escaped,
And for revenge will guide us. In reward
She asks her brother's forfeiture of lands
In marriage with Numacian : something too
Touching his life, that for her services
It might be spared, she said ;—an after-thought
To salve decorum, and if conscience wake
Serve as a sop : but when the sword shall smite

Pelayo and his dangerous race, I ween
That a thin kerchief will dry all the tears
That Lady Guisla sheds !
                              'Tis the old taint !
Said Julian mournfully ; from her mother's womb
She brought the inbred wickedness which now
In ripe infection blossoms. Woman, woman,
Still to the Goths art thou the instrument
Of overthrow ; thy virtue and thy vice
Fatal alike to them !
                        Say, rather, cried
The insidious renegade, that Allah thus
By woman punisheth the idolatry
Of those who raise a woman to the rank
Of godhead, calling on their Mary's name
With senseless prayers. In vain shall they invoke
Her trusted succour now ! like silly birds
By fear betrayed, they fly into the toils ;
And this Pelayo, who in lengthened war
Baffling our force, has thought perhaps to reign
Prince of the mountains, when we hold his wife
And offspring at our mercy, must himself
Come to the lure.
                      Enough, the leader said ;
This unexpected work of favouring Fate
Opens an easy way to our desires,
And renders further counsel needless now.
Great is the Prophet, whose protecting power
Goes with the faithful forth ! the rebels' days
Are numbered ! Allah hath delivered them
Into our hands !
                    So saying, he arose ;
The chiefs withdrew, Orpas alone remained,
Obedient to his indicated will.
The event, said Abulcacem, hath approved
Thy judgment in all points ; his daughter comes
At the first summons, even as thou saidst ;
Her errand with the insurgents done, she brings
Their well concerted project back, a safe
And unexpected messenger ;—the Moor,
The shallow Moor,—must see and not perceive ;
Must hear and understand not ; yea, must bear,

Poor easy fool, to serve their after mirth,
A part in his own undoing !   But just Heaven
With this unlooked-for incident hath marred
Their complots, and the sword shall cut this web
Of treason.
           Well, the renegade replied,
Thou knowest Count Julian's spirit, quick in wiles,
In act audacious.   Baffled now, he thinks
Either by instant warning to apprise
The rebels of their danger, or preserve
The hostages when fallen into our power,
Till secret craft contrive, or open force
Win their enlargement.   Haply too he dreams
Of Cordoba, the avenger and the friend
Of Abdalazis, in that cause to arm
Moor against Moor, preparing for himself
The victory o'er the enfeebled conquerors.
Success in treason hath emboldened him,
And power but serves him for fresh treachery, false
To Roderick first, and to the Caliph now.

    The guilt, said Abulcacem, is confirmed,
The sentence passed : all that is now required
Is to strike sure and safely.   He hath with him
A veteran force devoted to his will,
Whom to provoke were perilous ; nor less
Of peril lies there in delay : what course
Between these equal dangers should we steer ?

They have been trained beneath him in the wars
Of Africa, the renegade replied ;
Men are they who, from their youth up, have found
Their occupation and their joy in arms ;
Indifferent to the cause for which they fight,
But faithful to their leader, who hath won
By licence largely given, yet tempered still
With exercise of firm authority,
Their whole devotion.   Vainly should we seek
By proof of Julian's guilt to pacify
Such martial spirits, unto whom all creeds
And countries are alike ; but take away
The head, and forthwith their fidelity

Goes at the market price. The act must be
Sudden and secret ; poison is too slow,
Thus it may best be done : the mountaineers,
Doubtless, ere long will rouse us with some spur
Of sudden enterprise ; at such a time
A trusty minister approaching him
May smite him, so that all shall think the spear
Comes from the hostile troops.

                      Right counsellor !
Cried Abulcacem, thou shalt have his lands,
The proper meed of thy fidelity :
His daughter thou mayst take or leave. Go now,
And find a faithful instrument to put
Our purpose in effect !—And when 'tis done,
The Moor, as Orpas from the tent withdrew,
Muttering pursued,—look for a like reward
Thyself ! that restless head of wickedness
In the grave will brood no treasons. Other babes
Scream when the devil, as they spring to life,
Infects them with his touch ; but thou didst stretch
Thine arms to meet him, and like mother's milk
Suck the congenial evil ! Thou hast tried
Both laws, and were there aught to gain, wouldst
    prove
A third as readily ; but when thy sins
Are weighed, 'twill be against an empty scale,
And neither Prophet will avail thee then !

XXIII.

THE VALE OF COVADONGA.

THE camp is stirring, and ere day hath dawned
The tents are struck. Early they rise whom hope
Awakens, and they travel fast with whom
She goes companion of the way. By noon
Hath Albucacem in his speed attained
The vale of Cangas. Well the trusty scouts
Observe his march, and fleet as mountain roes,
From post to post with instantaneous speed

The warning bear : none else is nigh ; the vale
Hath been deserted, and Pelayo's hall
Is open to the foe, who on the tower
Hoist their white signal-flag. In Sella's stream
The misbelieving multitudes perform,
With hot and hasty hand, their noontide rite,
Then hurryingly repeat the Impostor's prayer.
Here they divide ; the chieftain halts with half
The host, retaining Julian and his men,
Whom where the valley widened he disposed,
Liable to first attack, that so the deed
Of murder planned with Orpas might be done.
The other force the Moor Alcahman led,
Whom Guisla guided up Pionia's stream
Eastward to Soto. Ibrahim went with him,
Proud of Granada's snowy heights subdued,
And boasting of his skill in mountain war ;
Yet sure he deemed an easier victory
Awaited him this day. Little, quoth he,
Weens the vain mountaineer who puts his trust
In dens and rocky fastnesses, how close
Destruction is at hand ! Belike he thinks
The Humma's happy wings have shadowed him,
And therefore Fate with royalty must crown
His chosen head ! Pity the scimitar
With its rude edge so soon should interrupt
The pleasant dream !
         There can be no escape
For those who in the cave seek shelter, cried
Alcahman ; yield they must, or from their holes
Like bees we smoke them out. The chief perhaps
May reign a while king of the wolves and bears,
Till his own subjects hunt him down, or kites
And crows divide what hunger may have left
Upon his ghastly limbs. Happier for him
That destiny should this day to our hands
Deliver him ; short would be his sufferings then ;
And we right joyfully should in one hour
Behold our work accomplished, and his race
Extinct.
         Thus these in mockery and in thoughts
Of bloody triumph, to the future blind,

Indulged the scornful vein; nor deemed that they
Whom to the sword's unsparing edge they doomed,
Even then in joyful expectation prayed
To Heaven for their approach, and at their post
Prepared, were trembling with excess of hope.
Here in these mountain straits the mountaineer
Had felt his country's strength insuperable;
Here he had prayed to see the Mussulman
With all his myriads; therefore had he looked
To Covadonga as a sanctuary
Apt for concealment, easy of defence;
And Guisla's flight, though to his heart it sent
A pang more poignant for their mother's sake,
Yet did it further in its consequence
His hope and project, surer than decoy
Well-laid, or best-concerted stratagem.
That sullen and revengeful mind, he knew,
Would follow to the extremity of guilt
Its long fore-purposed shame: the toils were laid,
And she who by the Mussulmans full sure
Thought on her kindred her revenge to wreak,
Led the Moors in.
                    Count Pedro and his son
Were hovering with the main Asturian force
In the wider vale to watch occasion there,
And with hot onset when the alarm began
Pursue the vantage.   In the fatal straits
Of Deva had the King disposed the rest:
Amid the hanging woods, and on the cliffs,
A long mile's length on either side its bed,
They lay.   The lever and the axe and saw
Had skilfully been plied; and trees and stones,
A dread artillery, ranged on crag and shelf
And steep descent, were ready at the word
Precipitate to roll resistless down.
The faithful maiden not more wistfully
Looks for the day that brings her lover home;—
Scarce more impatiently the horse endures
The rein, when loud and shrill the hunter's horn
Rings in his joyous ears, than at their post
The mountaineers await their certain prey;
Yet mindful of their Prince's order, oft

And solemnly enforced, with eagerness
Subdued by minds well-mastered, they expect
The appointed signal.
                Hand must not be raised,
Foot stirred, nor voice be uttered, said the chief,
Till the word pass : impatience would mar all.
God hath delivered over to your hands
His enemies and ours, so we but use
The occasion wisely.   Not till the word pass
From man to man transmitted, " In the name
Of God, for Spain and vengeance ! " let a hand
Be lifted ; on obedience all depends,
Their march below with noise of horse and foot
And haply with the clang of instruments,
Might drown all other signal, this is sure ;
But wait it calmly ; it will not be given
Till the whole line hath entered in the toils.
Comrades, be patient, so shall none escape
Who once set foot within these straits of death.
Thus had Pelayo on the mountaineers
With frequent and impressive charge enforced
The needful exhortation.   This alone
He doubted, that the Mussulmans might see
The perils of the vale, and warily
Forbear to enter.   But they thought to find,
As Guisla told, the main Asturian force
Seeking concealment there, no other aid
Soliciting from these their native hills ;
And that the babes and women having fallen
In thraldom, they would lay their weapons down,
And supplicate forgiveness for their sake.
Nor did the Moors perceive in what a strait
They entered ; for the morn had risen o'ercast,
And when the sun had reached the height of Heaven,
Dimly his pale and beamless orb was seen
Moving through mist.   A soft and gentle rain,
Scarce heavier than the summer's evening dew,
Descended,—through so still an atmosphere,
That every leaf upon the moveless trees
Was studded o'er with rain-drops, bright and full,
None falling till from its own weight o'erswoln
The motion came.

Low on the mountain side
The fleecy vapour hung, and in its veil
With all their dreadful preparations wrapped
The mountaineers ;—in breathless hope they lay,
Some blessing God in silence for the power
This day vouchsafed ; others with fervency
Of prayer and vow invoked the Mother-Maid,
Beseeching her that in this favouring hour
She would be strongly with them.   From below
Meantime distinct they heard the passing tramp
Of horse and foot, continuous as the sound
Of Deva's stream, and barbarous tongues commixt
With laughter, and with frequent shouts,—for all
Exultant came, expecting sure success ;
Blind wretches, over whom the ruin hung !

They say, quoth one, that though the Prophet's
      soul
Doth with the black-eyed houris bathe in bliss,
Life hath not left his body, which bears up
By its miraculous power the holy tomb,
And holds it at Medina in the air
Buoyant between the temple's floor and roof :
And there the angels fly to him with news
From east, west, north, and south, of what befalls
His faithful people.   If when he shall hear
The tale of this day's work, he should for joy
Forget that he is dead, and walk abroad,—
It were as good a miracle as when
He sliced the moon !   Sir Angel hear me now,
Whoe'er thou be'st who art about to speed
From Spain to Araby ! when thou hast got
The Prophet's ear, be sure thou tellest him
How bravely Ghauleb did his part to-day,
And with what special reverence he alone
Desired thee to commend him to his grace !—
Fie on thee, scoffer that thou art ! replied
His comrade ; thou wilt never leave these gibes
Till some commissioned arrow through the teeth
Shall nail the offending tongue.   Hast thou not
      heard
How when our clay is leavened first with life,

The ministering angel brings it from that spot
Whereon 'tis written in the eternal book
That soul and body must their parting take,
And earth to earth return? How knowest thou
But that the spirit who compounded thee,
To distant Syria from this very vale
Bore thy component dust, and Azrael here
Awaits thee at this hour?—Little thought he
Who spake that in that valley at that hour
One death awaited both!
                              Thus they pursued
Toward the cave their inauspicious way.
Weak childhood there and ineffective age
In the chambers of the rock were placed secure;
But of the women, all whom with the babes
Maternal care detained not, were aloft
To aid in the destruction; by the side
Of fathers, brethren, husbands, stationed there
They watch and pray. Pelayo in the cave
With the venerable primate took his post.
Ranged on the rising cliffs on either hand
Vigilant sentinels with eye intent
Observe his movements, when to take the word
And pass it forward. He in arms complete
Stands in the portal: a stern majesty
Reigned in his countenance severe that hour,
And in his eye a deep and dreadful joy
Shone, as advancing up the vale he saw
The Moorish banners. God hath blinded them!
He said; the measure of their crimes is full!
O Vale of Deva, famous shalt thou be
From this day forth for ever; and to these
Thy springs shall unborn generations come
In pilgrimage, and hallow with their prayers
The cradle of their native monarchy!

There was a stirring in the air, the sun
Prevailed, and gradually the brightening mist
Began to rise and melt. A jutting crag
Upon the right projected o'er the stream,
Not farther from the cave than a strong hand
Expert, with deadly aim, might cast the spear,

Or a strong voice, pitched to full compass, make
Its clear articulation heard distinct.
A venturous dalesman, once ascending there
To rob the eagle's nest, had fallen, and hung
Among the heather, wondrously preserved :
Therefore had he with pious gratitude
Placed on that overhanging brow a cross,
Tall as the mast of some light fisher's skiff,
And from the vale conspicuous. As the Moors
Advanced, the chieftain in the van was seen
Known by his arms, and from the crag a voice
Pronounced his name,—Alcahman ! hoa, look up,
Alcahman ! As the floating mist drew up,
It had divided there, and opened round
The cross ; part clinging to the rock beneath,
Hovering and waving part in fleecy folds,
A canopy of silver light condensed
To shape and substance. In the midst there
       stood
A female form, one hand upon the cross,
The other raised in menacing act ; below
Loose flowed her raiment, but her breast was
       armed,
And helmeted her head. The Moor turned pale,
For on the walls of Auria he had seen
That well-known figure, and had well believed
She rested with the dead. What, hoa ! she cried,
Alcahman ! In the name of all who fell
At Auria in the massacre, this hour
I summon thee before the throne of God
To answer for the innocent blood ! This hour,
Moor, miscreant, murderer, child of hell, this hour
I summon thee to judgment !—In the name
Of God ! for Spain and vengeance !
                              Thus she closed
Her speech ; for taking from the Primate's hand
That oaken cross which at the sacring rites
Had served for crosier, at the cavern's mouth
Pelayo lifted it and gave the word.
From voice to voice on either side it passed
With rapid repetition,—In the name
Of God ! for Spain and vengeance ! and forthwith

On either side along the whole defile
The Asturians shouting in the name of God,
Set the whole ruin loose ! huge trunks and stones,
And loosened crags, down down they rolled with
    rush
And bound, and thundering force. Such was the
    fall
As when some city by the labouring earth
Heaved from its strong foundations, is cast down,
And all its dwellings, towers, and palaces,
In one wide desolation prostrated.
From end to end of that long strait, the crash
Was heard continuous, and commixed with sounds
More dreadful, shrieks of horror and despair,
And death,—the wild and agonising cry
Of that whole host in one destruction whelmed.
Vain was all valour there, all martial skill ;
The valiant arm is helpless now ; the feet
Swift in the race avail not now to save ;
They perish, all their thousands perish there,—
Horsemen and infantry they perish all,—
The outward armour and the bones within
Broken and bruised and crushed. Echo prolonged
The long uproar ; a silence then ensued,
Through which the sound of Deva's stream was
    heard,
A lonely voice of waters, wild and sweet ;
The lingering groan, the faintly-uttered prayer,
The louder curses of despairing death,
Ascended not so high. Down from the cave
Pelayo hastes, the Asturians hasten down,
Fierce and immitigable down they speed
On all sides, and along the vale of blood
The avenging sword did mercy's work that hour.

XXIV.

RODERICK AND COUNT JULIAN.

THOU hast been busy, Death! this day, and yet
But half thy work is done; the gates of hell
Are thronged, yet twice ten thousand spirits more,
Who from their warm and healthful tenements
Fear no divorce, must ere the sun go down
Enter the world of woe! the gate of Heaven
Is open too, and angels round the throne
Of mercy on their golden harps this day
Shall sing the triumphs of redeeming love.

There was a church at Cangas dedicate
To that apostle unto whom his Lord
Had given the keys; a humble edifice,
Whose rude and time-worn structure suited well
That vale among the mountains. Its low roof
With stone plants and with moss was overgrown,
Short fern, and richer weeds which from the eaves
Hung their long tresses down. White lichens
        clothed
The sides, save where the ivy spread, which bowered
The porch, and clustering round the pointed wall,
Wherein two bells, each open to the wind,
Hung side by side, threaded by hairy shoots
The double niche; and climbing to the cross,
Wreathed it and half-concealed its sacred form
With bushy tufts luxuriant. Here in the font,—
Borne hither with rejoicing and with prayers
Of all the happy land who saw in him
The lineage of their ancient chiefs renewed,—
The Prince had been immersed: and here within
An oaken galilee, now black with age,
His old Iberian ancestors were laid.

Two stately oaks stood nigh, in the full growth
Of many a century. They had flourished there
Before the Gothic sword was felt in Spain,
And when the ancient sceptre of the Goths

Was broken, there they flourished still.   Their
    boughs
Mingled on high, and stretching wide around,
Formed a deep shade, beneath which canopy
Upon the ground Count Julian's board was spread,
For to his daughter he had left his tent
Pitched for her use hard by.   He at the board
Sate with his trusted captains, Gunderick,
Felix and Miro, Theudered and Paul,
Basil and Cottila, and Virimar,
Men through all fortunes faithful to their lord,
And to that old and tried fidelity,
By personal love and honour held in ties
Strong as religious bonds.   As there they sate,
In the distant vale a rising dust was seen,
And frequent flash of steel,—the flying fight
Of men who, by a fiery foe pursued
Put forth their coursers at full speed, to reach
The aid in which they trust.   Up sprang the chiefs,
And hastily taking helm and shield, and spear,
Sped to their post.
                    Amid the chestnut groves
On Sella's side, Alphonso had in charge
To watch the foe ; a prowling band came nigh,
Whom with the ardour of impetuous youth
He charged and followed them in close pursuit :
Quick succours joined them ; and the strife grew hot,
Ere Pedro hastening to bring off his son,
Or Julian and his captains,—bent alike
That hour to abstain from combat (for by this
Full sure they deemed Alcahman had secured
The easy means of certain victory),—
Could reach the spot.   Both thus in their intent
According, somewhat had they now allayed
The fury of the fight, though spears still flew
And strokes of sword and mace were interchanged,
When passing through the troop a Moor came up
On errand from the chief, to Julian sent ;
A fatal errand fatally performed
For Julian, for the chief, and for himself,
And all that host of Mussulmans he brought ;
For while with well dissembled words he lured

The warrior's ear, the dexterous ruffian marked
The favouring moment and unguarded place,
And plunged a javelin in his side. The Count,
Fell, but in falling called to Cotila,
Treachery! the Moor! the Moor!—He too on
   whom
He called had seen the blow from whence it came,
And seized the murderer. Miscreant! he exclaimed,
Who set thee on? The Mussulman, who saw
His secret purpose baffled, undismayed,
Replies, What I have done is authorised;
To punish treachery and prevent worse ill
Orpas and Albucacem sent me here;
The service of the Caliph and the Faith
Required the blow.
               The Prophet and the Fiend
Reward thee then! cried Cottila; meantime
Take thou from me thy proper earthly meed:
Villain!—and lifting as he spake the sword,
He smote him on the neck: the trenchant blade
Through vein and artery passed and yielding bone,
And on the shoulder, as the assassin dropped,
His head half-severed fell. The curse of God
Fall on the Caliph and the Faith and thee!
Stamping for anguish, Cottila pursued;
African dogs, thus is it ye requite
Our services?—But dearly shall ye pay
For this day's work!—O fellow-soldiers, here,
Stretching his hands toward the host, he cried,
Behold your noble leader basely slain!
He who for twenty years hath led us forth
To war, and brought us home with victory,
Here he lies foully murdered,—by the Moors,—
Those whom he trusted, whom he served so well!
Our turn is next! but neither will we wait
Idly, nor tamely fall!
               Amid the grief,
Tumult, and rage, of those who gathered round,
When Julian could be heard, I have yet life,
He said, for vengeance. Virimar, speed thou
To yonder mountaineers, and tell their chiefs
That Julian's veteran army joins this day

Pelayo's standard !   The command devolves
On Gunderick.   Fellow-soldiers, who so well
Redressed the wrongs of your old general,
Ye will not let his death go unrevenged !—
Tears then were seen on many an iron cheek,
And groans were heard from many a resolute heart,
And vows with imprecations mixed went forth,
And curses checked by sobs.   Bear me apart,
Said Julian, with a faint and painful voice,
And let me see my daughter ere I die.

Scarce had he spoken when the pitying throng
Divide before her.   Eagerly she came ;
A deep and fearful lustre in her eye,
A look of settled woe,—pale, deadly pale,
Yet to no lamentations giving way,
Nor tears nor groans ;—within her breaking heart
She bore the grief, and kneeling solemnly
Beside him, raised her awful hands to heaven,
And cried, Lord God ! be with him in this hour !
Two things have I to think of, O my child,
Vengeance and thee, said Julian.   For the first
I have provided : what remains of life
As best may comfort thee may so be best
Employed ; let me be borne within the church,
And thou, with that good man who follows thee,
Attend me there.
                        Thus when Florinda heard
Her father speak, a gleam of heavenly joy
Shone through the anguish of her countenance.
O gracious God, she cried, my prayers are heard ;
Now let me die !—They raised him from the earth ;
He, knitting as they lifted him his brow,   .
Drew in through open lips and teeth firm-closed
His painful breath, and on the lance laid hand,
Lest its long shaft should shake the mortal
        wound.
Gently his men with slow and steady step
Their suffering burthen bore, and in the church
Before the altar laid him down, his head
Upon Florinda's knees.—Now, friends, said he,
Farewell.   I ever hoped to meet my death

Among ye, like a soldier,—but not thus !
Go join the Asturians ; and in after years,
When of your old commander ye shall talk,
How well he loved his followers, what he was
In battle, and how basely he was slain,
Let not the tale its fit completion lack,
But say how bravely was his death revenged.
Vengeance ! in that good word doth Julian make
His testament ; your faithful swords must give
The will its full performance. Leave me now,
I have done with worldly things. Comrades, fare-
    well,
And love my memory !
                    They with copious tears
Of burning anger, grief exasperating
Their rage, and fury giving force to grief,
Hastened to form their ranks against the Moors.
Julian meantime toward the altar turned
His languid eyes : That image, is it not
St. Peter, he inquired, he who denied
His Lord and was forgiven ?—Roderick rejoined,
It is the Apostle ; and may that same Lord,
O Julian, to thy soul's salvation bless
The seasonable thought !
                    The dying Count
Then fixed upon the Goth his earnest eyes.
No time, said he, is this for bravery,
As little for dissemblance. I would fain
Die in the faith wherein my fathers died,
Whereto they pledged me in mine infancy.—
A soldier's habits, he pursued, have steeled
My spirit, and perhaps I do not fear
This passage as I ought. But if to feel
That I have sinned, and from my soul renounce
The Impostor's faith, which never in that soul
Obtained a place,—if at the Saviour's feet,
Laden with guilt, to cast myself and cry,
Lord, I believe ! help Thou my unbelief !—
If this in the sincerity of death
Sufficeth,—Father, let me from thy lips
Receive the assurances with which the Church
Doth bless the dying Christian.

                              Roderick raised
His eyes to Heaven, and crossing on his breast
His open palms, Mysterious are Thy ways
And merciful, O gracious Lord! he cried,
Who to this end hast thus been pleased to lead
My wandering steps!   O Father, this Thy son
Hast sinned and gone astray : but hast not Thou
Said, When the sinner from his evil ways
Turneth, that he shall save his soul alive,
And angels at the sight rejoice in Heaven?
Therefore do I, in Thy most holy name,
Into Thy family receive again
Him who was lost, and in that name absolve
The penitent.—So saying, on the head
Of Julian solemnly he laid his hands.
Then to the altar tremblingly he turned,
And took the bread, and breaking it, pursued,
Julian ! receive from me the bread of life !
In silence reverently the Count partook
The reconciling rite, and to his lips
Roderick then held the consecrated cup.

   Me too ! exclaimed Florinda, who till then
Had listened speechlessly !   Thou man of God,
I also must partake !   The Lord hath heard
My prayers ! one sacrament, — one hour, — one
      grave,—
One resurrection !
                         That dread office done,
Count Julian with amazement saw the priest
Kneel down before him.   By the sacrament
Which we have here partaken, Roderick cried,
In this most awful moment ; by that hope,—
That holy faith which comforts thee in death,
Grant thy forgiveness, Julian, ere thou diest !
Behold the man who most hath injured thee !
Roderick, the wretched Goth, the guilty cause
Of all thy guilt,—the unworthy instrument
Of thy redemption,—kneels before thee here,
And prays to be forgiven !
                             Roderick ! exclaimed
The dying Count,—Roderick !—and from the floor

With violent effort half he raised himself;
The spear hung heavy in his side, and pain
And weakness overcame him, that he fell
Back on his daughter's lap. O Death! cried he,—
Passing his hand across his cold damp brow,—
Thou tamest the strong limb, and conquerest
The stubborn heart! But yesterday I said
One heaven could not contain mine enemy
And me : and now I lift my dying voice
To say, Forgive me, Lord, as I forgive.
Him who hath done the wrong!—He closed his
    eyes
A moment; then with sudden impulse cried,—
Roderick, thy wife is dead,—the Church hath power
To free thee from thy vows,—the broken heart
Might yet be healed, the wrong redressed, the throne
Rebuilt by that same hand which pulled it down,
And these cursed Africans—Oh, for a month
Of that waste life which millions misbestow!—
His voice was passionate, and in his eye
With glowing animation while he spake
The vehement spirit shone : its effort soon
Was past, and painfully with feeble breath
In slow and difficult utterance he pursued,—
Vain hope, if all the evil was ordained,
And this wide wreck the will and work of Heaven,
We but the poor occasion! Death will make
All clear, and joining us in better worlds,
Complete our union there! Do for me now
One friendly office more :—Draw forth the spear,
And free me from this pain!—Receive his soul,
Saviour! exclaimed the Goth, as he performed
The fatal service. Julian cried, O friend!—
True friend!—and gave to him his dying hand.
Then said he to Florinda, I go first,
Thou followest!—kiss me, child!—and now good
    night!
When from her father's body she arose,
Her cheek was flushed, and in her eyes there beamed
A wilder brightness. On the Goth she gazed,
While underneath the emotions of that hour
Exhausted life gave way. O God! she said,

Lifting her hands, thou hast restored me all,—
All—in one hour !—and round his neck she threw
Her arms and cried, My Roderick! mine in Heaven!
Groaning, he clasped her close, and in that act
And agony her happy spirit fled.

—⚬⚭⚬—

XXV.

RODERICK IN BATTLE.

EIGHT thousand men had to Asturias marched
Beneath Count Julian's banner ; the remains
Of that brave army which in Africa
So well against the Mussulman made head,
Till sense of injuries insupportable,
And raging thirst of vengeance, overthrew
Their leader's noble spirit.   To revenge
His quarrel, twice that number left their bones,
Slain in unnatural battle, on the field
Of Xeres, when the sceptre from the Goths
By righteous Heaven was reft.   Others had fallen
Consumed in sieges, alway by the Moor
To the front of war opposed.   The policy,
With whatsoever show of honour cloaked,
Was gross, and this surviving band had oft
At their carousals, of the flagrant wrong
Held such discourse as stirs the mounting blood,
The common danger with one discontent
Affecting chiefs and men.   Nor had the bonds
Of rooted discipline and faith attached,
Thus long restrained them, had they not known we
That Julian in their just resentment shared,
And fixed their hopes on him.   Slight impulse now
Sufficed to make these fiery martialists
Break forth in open fury ; and though first
Count Pedro listened with suspicious ear
To Julian's dying errand, deeming it
Some new decoy of treason,—when he found
A second legate followed Virimar,
And then a third, and saw the turbulence

H 2

Of the camp, and how against the Moors in haste
They formed their lines, he knew that Providence
This hour for his country interposed,
And in such faith advanced to use the aid
Thus wondrously ordained.   The eager chiefs
Hasten to greet him, Cottila and Paul,
Basil and Miro, Theudered, Gunderick,
Felix, and all who held authority ;
The zealous services of their brave host
They proffered, and besought him instantly
To lead against the African their force
Combined, and in good hour assail a foe
Divided, nor for such attack prepared.

   While thus they communed, Roderick from the
     church
Came forth, and seeing Pedro, bent his way
Toward them.   Sirs, said he, the Count is dead ;
He died a Christian, reconciled to Heaven,
In faith ; and when his daughter had received
His dying breath, her spirit too took flight.
One sacrament, one death, united them ;
And I beseech ye, ye who from the work
Of blood which lies before us may return,—
If, as I think, it should not be my fate—
That in one grave with Christian ceremonies
Ye lay them side by side.   In Heaven I ween
They are met through mercy :—ill befall the man
Who should in death divide them !—Then he turned
His speech to Pedro in an under voice ;
The King, said he, I know with noble mind
Will judge of the departed ; Christian-like
He died, and with a manly penitence :
They who condemn him most should call to mind
How grievous was the wrong which maddened
     him ;
Be that remembered in his history,
And let no shame be offered his remains.

   As Pedro would have answered, a loud cry
Of menacing imprecation from the troops
Arose ; for Orpas, by the Moorish chief

Sent to allay the storm his villainy
Had stirred, came hastening on a milk-white steed,
And at safe distance having checked the rein
Beckoned for parley. 'Twas Orelio
On which he rode, Roderick's own battle-horse,
Who from his master's hand had wont to feed,
And with a glad docility obey
His voice familiar. At the sight the Goth
Started, and indignation to his soul
Brought back the thoughts and feelings of old times.
Suffer me, Count, he cried, to answer him,
And hold these back the while ! Thus having said,
He waited no reply, but as he was,
Bareheaded, and in his weeds, and all unarmed,
Advanced toward the renegade. Sir Priest,
Quoth Orpas as he came, I hold no talk
With thee ; my errand is with Gunderick
And the captains of the host, to whom I bring
Such liberal offers and clear proof—
                            The Goth,
Breaking with scornful voice his speech, exclaimed,
What, could no steed but Roderick's serve thy turn?
I should have thought some sleek and sober mule,
Long trained in shackles to procession pace,
More suited to my lord of Seville's use
Than this good war-horse,—he who never bore
A villain, until Orpas crossed his back !—
Wretch ! cried the astonished renegade, and
      stooped,
Foaming with anger, from the saddle-bow
To reach his weapon. Ere the hasty hand
Trembling in passion could perform its will,
Roderick had seized the reins. How now, he cried,
Orelio ! old companion,—my good horse,—
Off with this recreant burthen !—and with that
He raised his hand, and reared and backed the
      steed,
To that remembered voice and arm of power
Obedient. Down the helpless traitor fell
Violently thrown, and Roderick over him
Thrice led with just and unrelenting hand
The trampling hoofs. Go join Witiza now,

Where he lies howling, the avenger cried,
And tell him Roderick sent thee!
                    At that sight
Count Julian's soldiers and the Asturian host
Set up a shout, a joyful shout, which rang
Wide through the welkin.   Their exulting cry
With louder acclamation was renewed,
When from the expiring miscreant's neck they saw
That Roderick took the shield, and round his own
Hung it, and vaulted in the seat. My horse!
My noble horse! he cried, with flattering hand
Patting his high-arched neck! the renegade,
I thank him for't, hath kept thee daintily!
Orelio, thou art in thy beauty still,
Thy pride and strength! Orelio, my good horse,
Once more thou bearest to the field thy lord,
He who so oft hath fed and cherished thee,
He for whose sake, wherever thou wert seen,
Thou wert by all men honoured. Once again
Thou hast thy proper master! Do thy part
As thou wert wont; and bear him gloriously,
My beautiful Orelio,—to the last—
The happiest of his fields!—Then he drew forth
The scimitar, and waving it aloft,
Rode toward the troops; its unaccustomed shape
Disliked him; Renegade in all things! cried
The Goth, and cast it from him; to the chiefs
Then said, If I have done ye service here,
Help me, I pray you, to a Spanish sword!
The trustiest blade that e'er in Bilbilis
Was dipped, would not to-day be misbestowed
On this right hand!—Go some one, Gunderick cried,
And bring Count Julian's sword. Whoe'er thou
    art,
The worth which thou hast shown avenging him
Entitles thee to wear it. But thou goest
For battle unequipped;—haste there and strip
Yon villain of his armour!
                    Late he spake,
So fast the Moors came on. It matters not,
Replied the Goth; there's many a mountaineer,
Who in no better armour cased this day

Than his wonted leathern gipion, will be found
In the hottest battle, yet bring off untouched
The unguarded life he ventures.—Taking then
Count Julian's sword, he fitted round his wrist
The chain, and eyeing the elaborate steel
With stern regard of joy.   The African
Under unhappy stars was born, he cried,
Who tastes thy edge !—Make ready for the charge !
They come—they come !—On, brethren, to the
    field !—
The word is Vengeance !
                       Vengeance was the word ;
From man to man, and rank to rank it passed,
By every heart enforced, by every voice
Sent forth in loud defiance of the foe.
The enemy in shriller sounds returned
Their Akbar and the Prophet's trusted name.
The horsemen lowered their spears, the infantry
Deliberately with slow and steady step
Advanced ; the bow-strings twanged, and arrows
    hissed,
And javelins hurtled by.   Anon the hosts
Met in the shock of battle, horse and man
Conflicting ; shield struck shield, and sword and
    mace
And curtle-axe on helm and buckler rung ;
Armour was riven, and wounds were interchanged,
And many a spirit from its mortal hold
Hurried to bliss or bale.   Well did the chiefs
Of Julian's army in that hour support
Their old esteem ; and well Count Pedro there
Enhanced his former praise ; and by his side,
Rejoicing like a bridegroom in the strife,
Alphonso through the host of infidels
Bore on his bloody lance dismay and death.
But there was worse confusion and uproar,
Their wildest slaughter and dismay, where, proud
Of his recovered lord, Orelio plunged
Through thickest ranks, trampling beneath his feet
The living and the dead.   Where'er he turns
The Moors divide and fly.   What man is this,
Appalled they say, who to the front of war

Bareheaded offers thus his naked life?
Replete with power he is, and terrible,
Like some destroying angel! Sure his lips
Have drank of Kaf's dark fountain, and he comes
Strong in his immortality! Fly! fly!
They said, this is no human foe!—Nor less
Of wonder filled the Spaniards when they saw
How flight and terror went before his way,
And slaughter in his path. Behold, cries one,
With what command and knightly ease he sits
The intrepid steed, and deals from side to side
His dreadful blows! Not Roderick in his power
Bestrode with such command and majesty
That noble war-horse. His loose robe this day
Is death's black banner, shaking from its folds
Dismay and ruin. Of no mortal mould
Is he who in that garb of peace affronts
Whole hosts, and sees them scatter where he turns!
Auspicious Heaven beholds us, and some saint
Revisits earth!
                    Ay, cries another, Heaven
Hath ever with especial bounty blest
Above all other lands its favoured Spain;
Choosing her children forth from all mankind
For its peculiar people, as of yore
Abraham's ungrateful race beneath the Law.
Who knows not how on that most holy night
When peace on earth by angels was proclaimed,
The light which o'er the fields of Bethlehem shone
Irradiated whole Spain? not just displayed,
As to the shepherds, and again withdrawn;
All the long winter hours from eve till morn
Her forests and her mountains and her plains,
Her hills and valleys were embathed in light,
A light which came not from the sun or moon
Or stars, by secondary powers dispensed,
But from the fountain-springs, the Light of Light
Effluent. And wherefore should we not believe
That this may be some saint or angel, charged
To lead us to miraculous victory?
Hath not the Virgin Mother oftentimes
Descending, clothed in glory, sanctified

With feet adorable our happy soil ?—
Marked ye not, said another, how he cast
In wrath the unhallowed scimitar away,
And called for Christian weapon? Oh, be sure
This is the aid of Heaven! On, comrades, on!
A miracle to-day is wrought for Spain!
Victory and vengeance! Hew the miscreants down,
And spare not! hew them down in sacrifice!
God is with us! His saints are in the field!
Victory! miraculous victory!
                              Thus they
Inflamed with wild belief the keen desire
Of vengeance on their enemies abhorred,
The Moorish chief, meantime, o'erlooked the fight
From an eminence, and cursed the renegade
Whose counsels sorting to such ill effect
Had brought this danger on. Lo, from the east
Comes fresh alarm! a few poor fugitives
Well-nigh with fear exanimate came up,
From Covadonga flying, and the rear
Of that destruction, scarce with breath to tell
Their dreadful tale. When Abulcacem heard,
Stricken with horror, like a man bereft
Of sense he stood. O Prophet! he exclaimed,
A hard and cruel fortune hast thou brought
This day upon thy servant! Must I then
Here with disgrace and ruin close a life
Of glorious deeds! But how should man resist
Fate's irreversible decrees, or why
Murmur at what must be? They who survive
May mourn the evil which this day begins :
My part will soon be done!—Grief then gave way
To rage, and cursing Guisla, he pursued,
Oh that that treacherous woman were but here!
It were a consolation to give her
The evil death she merits!
                              That reward
She hath had, a Moor replied. For when we reached
The entrance of the vale, it was her choice
There in the farthest dwellings to be left,

Lest she should see her brother's face ; but thence
We found her flying at the overthrow,
And visiting the treason on her head,
Pierced her with wounds.—Poor vengeance for a
    host
Destroyed ! said Abulcacem in his soul.
Howbeit, resolving to the last to do
His office, he roused up his spirit.   Go,
Strike off Count Eudon's head ! he cried ; the
    fear
Which brought him to our camp will bring him
    else
In arms against us now ; for Sisibert
And Ebba, he continued thus in thought,
Their uncle's fate for ever bars all plots
Of treason on their part ; no hope have they
Of safety but with us.   He called them then
With chosen troops to join him in the front
Of battle, that by bravely making head,
Retreat might now be won.   Then fiercer raged
The conflict, and more frequent cries of death,
Mingling with imprecations and with prayers,
Rose through the din of war.
                        By this the blood
Which Deva down her fatal channel poured,
Purpling Pionia's course, had reached and stained
The wider stream of Sella.   Soon far off
The frequent glance of spears and gleam of arms
Were seen, which sparkled to the westering orb,
Where down the vale, impatient to complete
The glorious work so well that day begun,
Pelayo led his troops.   On foot they came,
Chieftains and men alike ; the oaken cross
Triumphant borne on high, precedes their march,
And broad and bright the argent banner shone.
Roderick, who dealing death from side to side,
Had through the Moorish army now made way,
Beheld it flash, and judging well what aid
Approached, with sudden impulse that way rode,
To tell of what had passed,—lest in the strife
They should engage with Julian's men, and mar
The mighty consummation.   One ran on

To meet him fleet of foot, and having given
His tale to this swift messenger, the Goth
Halted a while to let Orelio breathe.
Siverian, quoth Pelayo, if mine eyes
Deceive me not, yon horse, whose reeking sides
Are red with slaughter, is the same on whom
The apostate Orpas in his vauntery
Wont to parade the streets of Cordoba.
But thou shouldst know him best ; regard him well :
Is't not Orelio?
           Either it is he,
The old man replied, or one so like to him,
Whom all thought matchless, that similitude
Would be the greater wonder.   But behold,
What man is he who in that disarray
Doth with such power and majesty bestride
The noble steed, as if he felt himself
In his own proper seat?   Look how he leans
To cherish him ; and how the gallant horse
Curves up his stately neck, and bends his head,
As if again to court that gentle touch,
And answer to the voice which praises him.
Can it be Maccabee? rejoined the King,
Or are the secret wishes of my soul
Indeed fulfilled, and hath the grave given up
Its dead?—So saying, on the old man he turned
Eyes full of wide astonishment, which told
The incipient thought that for incredible
He spake no farther.   But enough had passed,
For old Siverian started at the words
Like one who sees a spectre, and exclaimed,
Blind that I was to know him not till now !
My master, O my master !
                He meantime
With easy pace moved on to meet their march.
King, to Pelayo he began, this day,
By means scarce less than miracle, thy throne
Is stablished, and the wrongs of Spain revenged.
Orpas the accursèd, upon yonder field
Lies ready for the ravens.   By the Moors
Treacherously slain, Count Julian will be found
Before Saint Peter's altar ; unto him

Grace was vouchsafed; and by that holy power
Which at Visonia from the Primate's hand
Of his own proper act to me was given,
Unworthy as I am,—yet sure I think
Not without mystery, as the event hath shown,—
Did I accept Count Julian's penitence,
And reconcile the dying man to Heaven.
Beside him hath his daughter fallen asleep;
Deal honourably with his remains, and let
One grave with Christian rites receive them both.
Is it not written that as the tree falls
So it shall lie?
          In this and all things else,
Pelayo answered, looking wistfully
Upon the Goth, thy pleasure shall be done.
Then Roderick saw that he was known, and turned
His head away in silence. But the old man
Laid hold upon his bridle, and looked up
In his master's face, weeping and silently.
Thereat the Goth with fervent pressure took
His hand, and bending down toward him, said,
My good Siverian, go not thou this day
To war! I charge thee keep thyself from harm!
Thou art past the age for battles, and with whom
Hereafter should thy mistress talk of me
If thou wert gone?—Thou seest I am unarmed;
Thus disarrayed as thou beholdest me,
Clean through yon miscreant army have I cut
My way unhurt; but being once by Heaven
Preserved, I would not perish with the guilt
Of having wilfully provoked my death.
Give me thy helmet and thy cuirass!—nay,—
Thou wert not wont to let me ask in vain,
Nor to gainsay me when my will was known!
To thee methinks I should be still the King.

   Thus saying, they withdrew a little way
Within the trees. Roderick alighted there,
And in the old man's armour dight himself.
Dost thou not marvel by what wondrous chance,
Said he, Orelio to his master's hand
Hath been restored? I found the renegade

Of Seville on his back, and hurled him down
Headlong to the earth.   The noble animal
Rejoicingly obeyed my hand to shake
His recreant burthen off, and trample out
The life which once I spared in evil hour.
Now let me meet Witiza's viperous sons
In yonder field, and then I may go rest
In peace,—my work is done !

And nobly done !
Exclaimed the old man.   Oh ! thou art greater now
Than in that glorious hour of victory
When grovelling in the dust Witiza lay,
The prisoner of thy hand !—Roderick replied,
O good Siverian, happier victory
Thy son hath now achieved,—the victory
Over the world, his sins and his despair.
If on the field my body should be found,
See it, I charge thee, laid in Julian's grave,
And let no idle ear be told for whom
Thou mournest.   Thou wilt use Orelio
As doth beseem the steed which hath so oft
Carried a king to battle ;—he hath done
Good service for his rightful lord to-day,
And better yet must do.   Siverian, now
Farewell !   I think we shall not meet again,
Till it be in that world where never change
Is known, and they who love shall part no more.
Commend me to my mother's prayers, and say
That never man enjoyed a heavenlier peace
Than Roderick at this hour.   O faithful friend
How dear thou art to me these tears may tell.

With that he fell upon the old man's neck ;
Then vaulted in the saddle, gave the reins,
And soon rejoined the host.   On, comrades, on !
Victory and vengeance ! he exclaimed, and took
The lead on that good charger, he alone
Horsed for the onset.   They with one consent
Gave all their voices to the inspiring cry,
Victory and vengeance ! and the hills and rocks
Caught the prophetic shout and rolled it round.
Count Pedro's people heard amid the heat

Of battle, and returned the glad acclaim.
The astonished Mussulmans, on all sides charged,
Hear that tremendous cry ; yet manfully
They stood, and everywhere with gallant front
Opposed in fair array the shock of war.
Desperately they fought, like men expert in arms,
And knowing that no safety could be found,
Save from their own right hands.   No former day
Of all his long career had seen their chief
Approved so well ; nor had Witiza's sons
Ever before this hour achieved in fight
Such feats of resolute valour.   Sisibert
Beheld Pelayo in the field afoot,
And twice essayed beneath his horse's feet
To thrust him down.   Twice did the Prince evade
The shock, and twice upon his shield received
The fratricidal sword.   Tempt me no more,
Son of Witiza, cried the indignant chief,
Lest I forget what mother gave thee birth !
Go meet thy death from any hand but mine,
He said, and turned aside.   Fitliest from me !
Exclaimed a dreadful voice, as through the throng
Orelio forced his way ; fitliest from me
Receive the rightful death too long withheld !
'Tis Roderick strikes the blow !   And as he spake,
Upon the traitor's shoulder fierce he drove
The weapon, well-bestowed.   He in the seat
Tottered and fell.   The avenger hastened on
In search of Ebba ; and in the heat of fight
Rejoicing and forgetful of all else,
Set up his cry as he was wont in youth,
Roderick the Goth !—His war-cry known so well.
Pelayo eagerly took up the word,
And shouted out his kinsman's name beloved,
Roderick the Goth !   Roderick and victory !
Roderick and vengeance !   Odoar gave it forth ;
Urban repeated it, and through his ranks
Count Pedro sent the cry.   Not from the field
Of his great victory, when Witiza fell,
With louder acclamations had that name
Been borne abroad upon the winds of Heaven.
The unreflecting throng, who yesterday,

If it had passed their lips, would with a curse
Have clogged it, echoed it as if it came
From some celestial voice in the air, revealed
To be the certain pledge of all their hopes.
Roderick the Goth! Roderick and victory!
Roderick and vengeance! O'er the field it spread,
All hearts and tongues uniting in the cry;
Mountains and rocks and vales re-echoed round;
And he, rejoicing in his strength, rode on,
Laying on the Moors with that good sword, and
      smote,
And overthrew, and scattered, and destroyed,
And trampled down; and still at every blow
Exultingly he sent the war-cry forth,
Roderick the Goth! Roderick and victory!
Roderick and vengeance!
                        Thus he made his way,
Smiting and slaying through the astonished ranks,
Till he beheld, where on a fiery barb,
Ebba, performing well a soldier's part,
Dealt to the right and left his deadly blows.
With mutual rage they met. The renegade
Displays a scimitar, the splendid gift
Of Walid from Damascus sent; its hilt
Embossed with gems, its blade of perfect steel,
Which, like a mirror sparkling to the sun
With dazzling splendour flashed. The Goth objects
His shield, and on its rim received the edge
Driven from its aim aside, and of its force
Diminished. Many a frustrate stroke was dealt
On either part, and many a foin and thrust
Aimed and rebated; many a deadly blow
Straight, or reverse, delivered and repelled.
Roderick at length with better speed hath reached
The apostate's turban, and through all its folds
The true Cantabrian weapon making way,
Attained his forehead. Wretch! the avenger cried,
It comes from Roderick's hand! Roderick the Goth,
Who spared, who trusted thee, and was betrayed!
Go tell thy father now how thou hast sped
With all thy treasons! Saying thus he seized
The miserable, who, blinded now with blood,

Reeled in the saddle ; and with sidelong step
Backing Orelio, drew him to the ground.
He shrieking, as beneath the horse's feet
He fell, forgot his late-learnt creed, and called
On Mary's name.   The dreadful Goth passed on,
Still plunging through the thickest war, and still
Scattering, where'er he turned, the affrighted ranks.

    Oh, who could tell what deeds were wrought
      that day,
Or who endure to hear the tale of rage,
Hatred, and madness, and despair, and fear,
Horror, and wounds, and agony, and death,
The cries, the blasphemies, the shrieks, and groans,
And prayers, which mingled with the din of arms
In one wild uproar of terrific sounds ;
While over all predominant was heard,
Reiterate from the conquerors o'er the field,
Roderick the Goth !   Roderick and victory !
Roderick and vengeance !—Woe for Africa !
Woe for the circumcised !   Woe for the faith
Of the lying Ishmaelite that hour !   The chiefs
Have fallen ; the Moors, confused and captainless,
And panic-stricken, vainly seek to escape
The inevitable fate.   Turn where they will,
Strong in his cause, rejoicing in success,
Insatiate at the banquet of revenge,
The enemy is there ; look where they will,
Death hath environed their devoted ranks ;
Fly where they will, the avenger and the sword
Await them,—wretches ! whom the righteous arm
Hath overtaken !—Joined in bonds of faith
Accursed, the most flagitious of mankind
From all parts met are here ; the apostate Greek,
The vicious Syrian, and the sullen Copt,
The Persian cruel and corrupt of soul,
The Arabian robber, and the prowling sons
Of Africa, who from their thirsty sands
Pray that the locusts on the peopled plain
May settle and prepare their way.   Conjoined
Beneath an impious faith, which sanctifies
To them all deeds of wickedness and blood,—

Yea, and halloos them on,—here are they met
To be conjoined in punishment this hour.
For plunder, violation, massacre,
All hideous, all unutterable things,
The righteous, the immitigable sword
Exacts due vengeance now! the cry of blood
Is heard, the measure of their crimes is full ;
Such mercy as the Moor at Auria gave,
Such mercy hath he found this dreadful hour !

The evening darkened, but the avenging sword
Turned not away its edge till night had closed
Upon the field of blood.   The chieftains then
Blew the recall, and from their perfect work
Returned rejoicing, all but he for whom
All looked with most expectance.   He full sure
Had thought upon that field to find his end
Desired, and with Florinda in the grave
Rest, in indissoluble union joined.
But still where through the press of war he went
Half-armed, and like a lover seeking death,
The arrows passed him by to right and left,
The spear-point pierced him not, the scimitar
Glanced from his helmet ; he, when he beheld
The rout complete, saw that the shield of Heaven
Had been extended over him once more,
And bowed before its will.   Upon the banks
Of Sella was Orelio found, his legs
And flanks incarnadined, his poitral smeared
With froth and foam and gore, his silver mane
Sprinkled with blood, which hung on every hair,
Aspersed like dew-drops ; trembling there he stood
From the toil of battle, and at times sent forth
His tremulous voice far echoing loud and shrill,
A frequent anxious cry, with which he seemed
To call the master whom he loved so well,
And who had thus again forsaken him.
Siverian's helm and cuirass on the grass
Lay near ; and Julian's sword, its hilt and chain
Clotted with blood ; but where was he whose
    hand
Had wielded it so well that glorious day ?—

Days, months, and years, and generations passed,
And centuries held their course, before, far off
Within a hermitage near Viseu's walls
A humble tomb was found, which bore inscribed
In ancient characters King Roderick's name.

THE END.

Printed by BALLANTYNE, HANSON & CO
Edinburgh and London

www.ingramcontent.com/pod-product-compliance
Lightning Source LLC
Chambersburg PA
CBHW031108020726
47495CB00007B/2102